Amie Barrodale

You Are Having a Good Time

CLANCY MARTIN

Amie Barrodale's stories and essays have appeared in *The Paris Review*, *Harper's Magazine*, *VICE*, *McSweeney's*, and other publications. In 2012 she was awarded *The Paris Review*'s Plimpton Prize for Fiction for her story "William Wei." She lives in Kansas City with her husband, the writer Clancy Martin.

You Are Having a Good Time

You Are Having a Good Time

STORIES

Amie Barrodale

Farrar, Straus and Giroux   New York

Farrar, Straus and Giroux
18 West 18th Street, New York 10011

Printed in the United States of America
First edition, 2016

The stories in this collection were originally published, in different form,
in *The Paris Review, Subtropics, Apology,* and *J&L Illustrated.*

Library of Congress Cataloging-in-Publication Data
Names: Barrodale, Amie.
Title: You are having a good time : stories / Amie Barrodale.
Description: First edition. | New York : Farrar, Straus and Giroux, 2016.
Identifiers: LCCN 2015035424 | ISBN 9780374293864 (softcover) |
    ISBN 9780374713294 (ebook)
Subjects: | BISAC: FICTION / Short Stories (single author).
Classification: LCC PS3602.A777543 A6 2016 | DDC 813/.6—dc23
LC record available at http://lccn.loc.gov/2015035424

Designed by Jonathan D. Lippincott

Our books may be purchased in bulk for promotional, educational, or business
use. Please contact your local bookseller or the Macmillan Corporate and
Premium Sales Department at 1-800-221-7945, extension 5442, or by e-mail at
MacmillanSpecialMarkets@macmillan.com.

www.fsgbooks.com • www.fsgoriginals.com
www.twitter.com/fsgbooks • www.facebook.com/fsgbooks

10 9 8 7 6 5 4 3 2 1

for Clancy

There is no such thing as communication. There are only two things. There is a successful miscommunication, and unsuccessful miscommunication. And when you have unsuccessful miscommunication, you are having a good time.

—Dzongsar Jamyang Khyentse Rinpoche

Contents

You Are Having a Good Time

William Wei

I once brought a girl home because I liked her shoes. That was the only thing I noticed about her. I live in a really small apartment. A lot of my clothes end up piled on my mattress or draped over the open door of the microwave. I guess the girl with the pink high heels woke up in the middle of the night and forgot where she was. She went out into the hallway naked and closed the door behind her. She told me later that she had asked me, and I told her that was the way to the bathroom, to go out the front door. I don't remember doing that. I remember I woke up with the cops in my house, asking me if I knew this girl. I said of course, she was the girl with the pink high heels. They thought that was really funny. After that, I didn't drink for about five months. I was mostly celibate, except for my upstairs neighbor, until she moved away. She was this Indian girl. She liked to do it from behind, in this one position. That was the only thing she wanted to do. The other things were boring, she said. When I went to the shower, she got up on all fours to masturbate.

I was alone for a while after that. I got rid of everything in my apartment. I worked ten- and twelve-hour days. Each night, I went to hot yoga. They had a studio between my home and work, on the fifteenth floor of this building, so that, across from you, while you were sweating, you could look in at people living their lives and see all these slow-moving domestic scenes, like a man standing in front of a microwave. After yoga, I liked to walk home. I liked the cold. I bought a Mediterranean-style salad from the same place every night. The woman who worked there was Lebanese and studying to be a doctor. I ate my dinner in front of the TV, watching *The Departed*.

It was a weeknight around 10 p.m. the first time she called. I let it go to voicemail, because I wasn't expecting any call, but when I went to get the message, it was just quiet for a while, and then the person hung up. At that time, I slept on an army-style cot. I ate on it, too, lying down with the food under my face, in the posture of a dog. This was the posture I was in several days later, the fourth time she called, and I answered.

"Who's this?" I asked. She said, "It's Koko." "Koko? I don't know any Koko." "I saw you at a party; it was a long time ago." "Oh, so I gave you my number?" "No, I got it from one of your friends." "I don't understand." "He told me your name is William." "Who was he?" "I can't tell you that. He said I couldn't tell you that. He said he was only telling me because he's worried, you don't go out anymore. He said you just lie around watching the same movie and eating the same food." "That's a lie," I said. She said, "He said you do hot yoga." "I don't even know what that is," I said. "Hold on." I reached out an arm and put the movie on pause. I put the container of salad under my cot and propped myself up on my elbows. "What do you look like, anyway? Maybe I remember seeing you."

"I'm about forty-eight years old."

"No." I flipped over onto my back and put an arm over my eyes. "I can tell from your voice you're younger."

"I'm attached to a breathing machine."

"Okay, fine—don't tell me, look, I've got to go."

"What do you mean?"

"Just that kind of joke—I mean, everybody says stuff like that. Why can't you just tell me what you look like?"

"Okay," she said. She sounded shy now. She thought around and said, "I guess I'm normal looking."

"What's normal?"

"I'm twenty-five. I have my hair cut into bangs."

"Uh-huh."

"I don't want to say any more than that."

It was weird, because I looked at pornography pretty frequently at this point. It was even a problem, so that I would spend an hour looking for the most disgusting pictures I could find. Maybe disgusting is not the word. For example, I liked a short video where an older man was fucking a girl in the ass while he put a Blow Pop inside her. Then he stopped and put it into her ass. Then he put it into her mouth, and he started to fuck her again. But somehow this conversation . . .

We talked for a long time, more than an hour, until I got sleepy, so I started to fall asleep with her on the phone. The next night, around the same time, she called me again. I was really happy she did that. We had a nice conversation. She told me this story, how she used to prank-call a math teacher of hers in junior high. She did it so much, she figured out how to reprogram his outgoing message, using his two-digit remote-access code. She redid his outgoing greetings, said things that were explicitly sexual. Her teacher didn't understand technology or remote-access codes. He assumed someone was breaking into his house each day to rerecord his message. It filled him with fear and paranoia. He bought a dog. He had an alarm installed and got a prescription for sleeping pills. It was a long time—nearly a year—before the police identified Koko and got to the bottom of the mystery. I loved that. I have stories like that, too. I told her the thing I did to my video teacher at an arts festival, and the things I used to say to my science teacher and to the owner of this antique store called J. B. & Lowther. I said, "Why don't you come over here right now?" and she told me she lived five hours away by train.

She had a business selling old clothing on the Internet. She was a night owl. She stayed up until sunrise pretty frequently, working on her business. All the clothes had to be cleaned, pressed, tried on, photographed, and entered into her website. By this time I had seen a lot of photos of her body. She used herself as a model, and the way she did it was very artistic. I'm not just saying that because I cared about her; I worked with major fashion houses, so I know what I'm saying. She really was artistic about how she did it, even though she always chopped her own head off. She made it look exciting and interior, like she was a party of one. In fact, she had a lot of admirers on the Internet. It wasn't just gross men; it was women in fashion, too. That's how it happened we were at the same party.

"What party was it?" I asked. "I don't think there was any party."

"They had set up a small stage on the roof, with that carpet rubber as a stage. That foam stuff they put under carpets."

"I remember that. That was a terrible party."

"You looked really drunk."

"I think I was really sad; I wish you had come and talked to me."

"You were talking to some other girls. You were always talking to lots of girls. I didn't think you'd want to talk to me."

"I'm sure I wanted to."

I knew that she drank, and most nights she was talking to me, she was drunk and taking pills, but I didn't think anything about it. She never slurred, or got sloppy, but she did seem sometimes to check out. It was like her heart would go dead. It was one time when she was like this that she told me she had had other romances on the telephone. I said I didn't care about that. She said, "You don't understand; I'm a sociopath."

"What's that mean?"

"Hold on."

She was gone for a while, and when she came back, she said, "All I mean is, what if when you see me, you think I'm ugly?"

"I'm not going to think you're ugly."

"You've never even seen my face. I could be completely deformed."

"I don't care," I said. "I'd love you even if you were deformed."

I guess that was a mistake. After I said it, she got really quiet. Then she said something weird. She said, "All my life I've been looking for my man. I think I finally found you." I think that was the moment, for both of us, when we realized it wouldn't happen. It was the next day, I think, that she started to tell me something about her mother being sick, but I could tell she didn't want to talk about it. Besides, I had already bought a ticket.

On the train, I kept telling myself to just be myself. I had a prescription for a low-milligram antianxiety medication, as well as a mild beta blocker, and I kept going into the bathroom to take more—I wanted to get the mixture right. After I took a pill, I'd check myself in the mirror, and I'd always be surprised at what I found. I kept expecting to find a monster.

At the station I checked my phone, and she'd left me this message where she just said my whole name, William Wei. She sounded completely freaked out. I knew her pretty well by this time. I could tell from how she sounded, it took everything in her not to run.

She was waiting across the street from the terminal. Just standing there, in front of her old car. She had on a green army coat and paint-splattered corduroy pants; her features were something like I pictured—wide eyes, Frida Kahlo—but she was more beautiful than I expected her to be.

When I got over to her car, before I could say anything, she said, "Are you nervous?"

"Are you?"

"We'll go to my house and relax."

In the car ride, she kept switching the tapes in her tape deck, and peering at me while she did it. I could tell she didn't like what she was seeing, but I didn't know what to do. I thought she had already seen me. I thought I was the one who was permitted to feel some disappointment.

She lived on the top floor of a converted flour mill. The sleeping area was the size of an ordinary bedroom, divided from the main area by ten-foot industrial shelves full of record albums—the inventory from her brother's store. He was itinerant and sometimes wrote to her, asking her to sell so many feet of albums. Her bed was a queen-size mattress on the floor. She pointed to the rotary phone beside it and lifted her cat to introduce him by name. Then she led me through the center portion of the loft, past a sliding glass door that connected to another apartment, a place rented to someone named Douglas. He was gone for the weekend, and so I didn't think much about him.

I don't think I will describe her kitchen or her work area, except a photo on the fridge. It was of an old man in a top hat and tails. She told me that was Douglas. I was about to tell her a story that the photo reminded me of when she handed me a piece of banana bread, a glass of milk, and two pills.

"What're these?" I said.

"My mom sent them to me earlier in the week. Something about her bowels."

"What?"

"She can't have opiates."

"They're opium?"

"Percocet."

I ate the pills and broke the bread into pieces. What I wanted was for the two of us to go and sit by the window and listen to record albums and get soulful, but Koko turned on the TV and flipped through the channels until she found a documentary. When that was over, she got a couple more pills for us and found a medley on a different station. We got take-out from a delivery service, and around eleven, her hair had fallen down, and her cheek was resting on her hand so the top of her head just touched my shoulder. I still have the shirt I was wearing at that time. It's hanging in my closet. I turned on my side to look at her body, and she pretended to keep watching TV.

I said, "I like your shoes."

"Those?" She lifted her head and turned to look at her feet. "Those are ballet slippers."

"I like how you are wearing them as shoes."

"Everyone does that."

"Everyone does what?"

She shook her head lightly from side to side.

"Everyone does what?" I said.

"I travel business class." She pointed a finger in the air. "Un momento, por favor. Muchas gracias, señor."

She was singing along with the television, but I stopped her before the next line. I mean I kissed her. It was a bit like kissing a doll, or a timid old lady. I mean that she didn't kiss me back, but I don't know if you know this. That can be very attractive. Later, Koko and I were together in haze, and her shirt was off, and she told me how she often induced men to love her and then abandoned them. She said, "Didn't you notice how I forced this on you?" I said, "I don't know what you mean," and she said, "Yeah. That's what I'm telling you."

So that was where it ended. Or really, it ended in the car, the first time we looked at each other. I mean, she thought I was ugly, and I could see that. But the thing about a dark truth is it is indistinguishable from doubt. And so—since I couldn't just go home—I kept approaching the dark area. Not by anything I said, but by what I did, and by watching how she reacted. She was nice at times, but at others, when her kindness drew me in, she was sharp, and I spent the weekend confused. I kept thinking, "But she already saw my face."

The next morning I was buttoning my shirt in the mirror when Koko opened her eyes. She yawned and smiled at my reflection and said, "You have a nice face." Then she pushed herself up onto all fours and shifted her butt in the air. She rested her cheek sideways on her folded arms and said, "We should go and eat eggs."

I wonder why I didn't say anything to her then. Like, "Why are you putting your butt in the air?" I guess it was because I didn't know what was going on. I had gotten clammed up, by the stuff the night before. I was shaky from the pills.

The restaurant was walking distance away. It was one of

those local-ingredients places. It had polished stone floors, and the polish was so high that when the hostess led us into the dining room, I thought there was a step up, but there wasn't one. It was just a trick of the light.

"What're you doing?" Koko said.

"I thought it was a step."

"You were like," she galloped one leg in imitation.

Everything I did made her angry. After we had our omelets, she pointed to a place between two of her teeth and said, "What's that thing there?" I have a large filling between two of my teeth about where she was pointing, so I told her that—"It's a filling"—and she said, "I can see it when you talk."

We went for a walk around the neighborhood. It was starting to feel like spring. We crossed into a residential area. On the sidewalk, one leashed dog was meeting another dog, and he got so excited he lost his footing and fell down on his side. An old suburban house was up for sale, and we let ourselves into its backyard to have a look around. One of its windows had been broken from the inside, and the pane lay in four pieces in the soil of a flower bed. I brushed my hand against Koko's, and she whipped her head around and said, "Do you want to take mushrooms?"

"What?"

"I have ten."

They were mixed into chocolates. They had been given to her by a friend, a photographer for *Playboy*. She said that several times, *Playboy*. She ate two chocolates and I ate one, and then we split a fourth. We got into her bed, and when I opened my eyes an hour later, the world was brilliant, alien, and unformed, and Koko was talking on the phone in the voice of a transistor radio.

"I'm fucked up," she said. "I'm on mushrooms. I'm on drugs. Yes, he's here since Friday. No, I don't think so. No. Not anything like that. Hold on." She pushed the phone aside and said, "I'm talking to Douglas."

I was really confused, so I went to get some air. I stood up out of the bed and went to look out the window. I stuck my head out and looked down at the alley, where a homeless man was digging through the garbage for glass bottles. I was really messed up, so I couldn't remember what to do. I was trying to remember if it was proper to throw money down at him. Somehow, I knew it wasn't right, but I couldn't figure out why, so I leaned back into the apartment and went to find my wallet. I looked for it out in the front room, and then I remembered where I left it. Yes, I was thinking, it definitely was what you did: you threw the money down. That was when I realized that Koko had put the phone down, and she was crying. She had been explaining, for how long I am not sure, that her mother had cancer. She told me that her mother had cancer of the bowels. I tried to console her; I sat beside her and put an arm around her shoulders. She let me hold her for a second, and then she stood up, and in a moment, she had her keys, and a door slammed, and she was gone. The cat was doing a little dance with its claws, that dance that's somehow associated with cat sex, and I was alone on her bed. It wasn't until recently I realized that whole thing about her mother was a lie. Besides, when I was consoling her, I wasn't really consoling her at all.

Anyway, it was a long time before she came back. The sorts of things I thought during that time, while I sat there, I can never really say. It was heavy. I think that's what people say—it was a bad trip; it was heavy. I think I can safely say it changed my life.

Animals

It was called *The Imp.* Victor Vargas had written a note on the cover, in pencil. "Read this and call me when you're done." The note was beside a drawing of what looked like a plume of smoke. Later Libby saw that the smoke had a wild-eyed, mischievous face and multiple curled fists.

When she called, an English woman told her Victor was out. He returned the call in the middle of the night.

"Is this an okay time to talk? I haven't caught you sleeping?"

"I'm awake."

"Are you sure? What time is it there?"

"I don't know. I guess it's the middle of the night. All my clocks stopped because of the earthquake."

"Oh dear, Libby, you have to reset them. You have to keep a schedule, and you can't do that if you don't know the time. Let's see, it's eleven a.m. here, so it would be what time there? Three a.m. Are you ordinarily awake at three a.m.?"

"To be honest, I haven't been sleeping."

"Insomnia," he murmured. "I'm sorry to hear that. I know what it's like. I had insomnia for all of 1985. Where are you, anyway? Are you in bed?"

"I haven't gotten out of bed for two weeks. I just ended a relationship, not that I guess you want to hear about that kind of thing."

"Why wouldn't I want to hear about it?"

"Presumably you have more interesting, more relevant topics to attain to."

"Perfect!"

"What?"

"To attain to. I like that for Kate. Hold on, I want to jot that down." He laughed. "I caught you at the right time. I'm normally not awake this early, but I went to Japan a few weeks ago and my circadian rhythms are still out of sync."

She sat up and arranged the pillows. Victor Vargas was calling her in the middle of the night and talking about one of the leads in the script he'd sent. All her previous roles had been supporting, or ensemble casts.

"Why were you in Japan?"

"Oh, money. I was there to arrange funding on the movie. I hate the country, though. I walk into a restaurant and bust the floor. I'm not even kidding, Libby. I put my foot through the floor of a restaurant, it was the tatami, and of course they're Japanese, so they have to be polite about it. On our last morning, we had to get to the airport before dawn, and we decided to visit a shrine before heading off, but then we got turned around, so I went to ask a young policewoman directions, and she wouldn't tell me. I joined my traveling companion and said, 'I don't know why, but she won't tell me.' My traveling companion pointed at my crotch and said, 'It might have something to do with that.' My pants were unzipped and my penis was hanging out. Hey, Libby? I really loved you in Bob's last picture. I really think you're terrific."

Libby walked the cordless into the kitchen and got a bottle of wine out of the refrigerator. Victor Vargas was praising particulars of her face in complicated ways, as if they were choices she'd made.

"And your voice. There's something so unusual about your voice, and it isn't the accent, though I love your accent, Libby."

"My accent?"

"Well, it's subtle, but it is there—I hear it. It's Southern, right?"

"Houston, Texas—born and raised."

"Your whole life? What's that like?"

"Oh, you know. Texas. Blondes and big houses and things of that nature."

"Things of that nature."

"What?"

"Just another weird idiosyncratic line for Kate."

He asked her again what Texas was like. She described her apartment complex, and her mother, and admitted she'd never met her father. She told Victor Vargas about her mother's previous marriage and how it had ended. She told him the story of her mother's first husband shooting himself in the leg in a Sonic drive-in. "The car filled up with smoke, and he said, 'Don't worry, it went all the way through.'"

Then she told him how her mom slept a lot, and her earliest memories were of wandering around the apartment complex alone.

"I went into other apartments and got into their closets. I remember eating a jawbreaker off some closet floor. I had to tear it out of the carpet fuzz, because somebody'd already sucked on it. One day, some kids threw dirt into our house, and I was too young to close the door. Later I saw a movie, and kids were doing that, or someone was, and I finally understood why."

"*Close Encounters of the Third Kind.*"

"That's right!"

"Richard Dreyfuss, before he got so annoying." He was satisfied with himself for knowing, like a kid trying to impress her. He gossiped about Richard Dreyfuss. He said the actor had been misdiagnosed bipolar and suffered from lithium poisoning. "I spoke to him during one of his so-called rapid cycles—the man was bored. He's an overgrown child." He said Dreyfuss had been using an earpiece for his lines for more than twenty years. When she said, "Interesting," he laughed for a long time, and then he spoke bitterly about naturalistic acting. "He had most of his training at the synagogue."

"I had most of my training at the synagogue."

"Well." He communicated, in the silence, that she was a better actor and a better person than Richard Dreyfuss. And the funny thing was, she believed it.

The sky lightened—they must have been talking for three hours when he said, "What about the domestic violence?"

"The what?"

"It's in Act II, you read all of it?"

"I did, but I've been so out of it. Oh, you mean the party!"

"When her husband punches her in the face two times, Libby, yes. The party."

"Well, doesn't she ask for it?"

"I don't know, does she? Is she really asking to be hit?"

"She says, clear as day, you know, hit me again."

"There's a difference between wanting to be hit and asking to be hit again."

Libby cleared her throat.

Victor said, "I wondered if she'd slept with another man downstairs and was trying to allay her guilt by placing him in a position of doing worse."

"I didn't see that in the script."

"Of course. But if you're going to play her, these are questions you need to consider. You're going to want to read between the lines. Because I love you in Bob's films. I loved you in *Sentinel*, but I got the impression you were trading on charisma. I want the tricks and I want more. I need you to do the work. We want you to read from the party scene."

She realized he expected an answer. "You want me to play the part?"

"*I* want you to, yes. David, the studio head, wants me to go with a name actress, but I've told him that's all wrong for this picture. Kate is fragile, and she's confused, and a movie star isn't going to be able to inhabit that. It's one of those elusive qualities, fragility, isn't it? Quite a bit like intelligence. You can't hire an actor with a thirty-two IQ and tell him to play a scientist—there's a stupidity in his eyes, and no matter what kind of genius he is, that stupidity is going to be there. Fragility is much the same. If I hire some Hollywood movie star, I'm not going to get that true open gaze, the one you so naturally possess. I'm having difficulty explaining it to them in a way they can understand. They keep sending me videotapes of movie stars making puppy eyes."

He laughed. She wasn't sure what he meant when he said that she wasn't a movie star.

"Libby, you understand it because you're a genius at what you do. But these are idiots I'm dealing with. These are people who try to get reservations at a restaurant because they read about it in a magazine. That's what I'm talking about. I tell them I don't care if Jane Lake is signed on. You can't have Jane Lake playing Kate. Obviously not. We already have a doe-eyed star, for Judith, with Cynthia Wu. For Kate we need someone who's mousy, someone who's vulnerable, a person who's been through a lot in her life, and it shows in her body and on her face."

Mousy? She showed wear on her face? Everyone said she looked younger than she was.

Libby poured the rest of the wine into a glass. When she put the bottle back on the marble counter, the sound it made was distinctive, and Victor stopped mid-sentence. He couldn't possibly know what Libby was doing. But she was sure he did. They were both quiet. Libby brought the glass and went and lay down on the couch in her study.

Victor shifted gears.

"We need you to come into the studios to do a shoot. I

need to show them Libby and then show them Jane Lake, and they'll see it. But if we're going to win this, Libby, and I think we will, I need you to make my lines work. I know Bob is loose with his dialogue, and he doesn't mind some improvisation. I don't do that. An actress of Jane Lake's caliber doesn't do that. I need you rock solid. I need you to know my lines. If you have to say them a thousand times, do it. Do your homework. Don't walk in. One thing I hate, and I'm going to tell you right from the start, is seeing an actor over by the crafts table at four a.m. with a page from my script. And Libby? Don't get in the way of the scene. Don't get in my way."

"What do you mean?"

"This movie is a small movie. It's a realistic movie. It's about family life, and it's about middle-class life. It's set in the home, and it's about the received ideas that govern one woman's inner life in her home. She tells herself she loves her husband and he loves her, but she knows the truth, and when she observes herself thinking about the truth, she suppresses the thought. In this scene, she recognizes that. So don't let Libby get in the way of Kate."

"Well, wouldn't that be good? I mean, given what you told me about the vulnerability I bring to the part, if I were to put myself into it?"

"Uh-huh. No, that's not right. I'm going to interrupt you now and put Terry on the phone, and he's going to explain what we need to go forward."

The phone line was quiet for a full minute. Then Terry picked up a phone line.

"Libby? Terry. Yes, I'm handling all the callbacks for

Kate. I don't know if Vic's talked to you. Yes? Good. Well, let me tell you, Vic wants us to do all of the audition tape in a studio that isn't so echo-y, so we're flying all of you in. We need you out here Wednesday afternoon, two p.m. to two-thirty."

When they had made arrangements, Victor said, "Work on the lines, Libby. I want you for the part."

"Were you listening in?" Libby asked.

"I have a feeling about us, and my feelings are never wrong, so if it doesn't work on this picture, don't worry about it. You're a really good actor, and I'm sure I'll use you soon. Oh, and, Libby? Is it all right if I call you again sometime?"

He hung up the phone.

She made coffee and took her script to the attic. She read her lines out loud, dispassionately, all morning. Her throat started to get scratchy. She wrote her lines out in longhand, filling a spiral notebook. Then she sat and thought about Kate, and what she would have been feeling in the moment. At first she tried to remember bad relationships, being lied to, but then when she read her lines with those things in mind, she got distracted. She thought about the key emotion of the scene—she decided it was fear expressing itself as aggression, that it was fight or flight—and she tried to remember a time when she felt like fighting. She couldn't get it, so she took her puppy for a walk. The damned dog was half poodle, and even though it came from a breeder, it was starting to act like a puppy-mill dog. It always wanted to go into her space—to walk right in front of her legs. Before she realized it, she was kicking the dog! When she got home, she read the scene again, and it worked, simply like that—thinking about her puppy, she got as angry as an ordinary woman would get if she was beaten. Angry at her damned stupid puppy, she recited the one line over and over—"Why don't you do it again?"

A day after the retest, Victor called and said, "You blew Jane Lake out of the water."

"I got the part!"

"Well, close. It's all there, but you showed a little too much. Take a week. Try it again. Rephrase it. Make it simple and concrete so we can deal with it."

"I have another test?"

"A formality, to wrap things up. I'm sending a cameraman to you. You'll do it by video, and he'll mail it to us."

Three weeks became a month and a half. She tried to reassure herself. Her mother worried for her, and she reassured her.

"He said I all but have the part, so I believe I do. According to Victor, I blew Jane Lake out of the water. Those were his exact words. The last retest is a formality. He's a perfectionist, but he's not a sadist. I mean, he wouldn't say that and then take it back. I hear he sometimes takes thirty, forty takes, to get it right when an actor walks across the dance floor. It drives people crazy. He had one actress who supposedly broke into his apartment, but then I heard he didn't keep it locked and they were sleeping together at the time."

"Libby, we have another word for that in Houston."

"What?"

"We call them assholes."

When Victor finally called, the conversation was relaxed. He told her she'd misread some of his lines and he'd changed them to reflect her reading. He apologized for being finicky about his exact lines. He said, "It's the sort of thing a TV director would make you do." Libby said, "Well, I didn't see it that way, but I'm happy to go back to my initial reading," and Victor laughed. He read to her from Jung's *Red Book*. He asked Libby where she was sitting, and she said she was lying on the ground. He said, "Somehow I knew that." He told Libby she should watch *Star Wars*, and she told him to watch *La Jetée*. He said, "How did you know I've always refused to watch Chris Marker? I've seen every other trashy movie ever made."

He asked if she had any questions about the edits.

"I have one question. In Act Two, Scene Three, when Kate and Michael— The love scene. It says it'll show the actress, ah, performing fellatio on the actor. Isn't it a little unnecessary?"

"How do you mean?"

"I don't know, I don't have the screenplay in front of me."

He flipped through his pages and started reading aloud from the scene. "Michael, harried from work, still wearing his overcoat and carrying his attaché, closes the front door. Kate is sitting on the couch, watching TV and smoking a cigarette."

Libby said, "Please stop! I'll do whatever it says, but please don't read it to me."

"Good."

He sent a revision two days before she was supposed to fly

out. There wasn't a note in the envelope—it was just the script. It was printed on different-colored papers—white, blue, pink, green, and two shades of yellow. She flipped through it. He'd added some description to the sex scene. He'd gone into precise detail about the blow job and the cigarette. It felt like he was needling her, or making something private between them into art. She couldn't decide which.

Victor was the center of the universe on set. He had small, pale hands and dainty little feet in beat-up running shoes. His handshake was limp, and he didn't allow their hands to clasp. He barely grasped her fingers, then pulled his hand away.

He said, "It's so nice to finally clap eyes on you."

"It's nice to meet you," Libby said. "It's like a dream."

A chubby woman with gray hair at her right temple came up behind Victor, rolling an orange armchair, and Victor turned away from Libby and got down on his hands and knees to look at its wheels.

"Those are very nice," Victor said. "Those are all right."

Victor took off his glasses and lay down to examine the wheels at close range. "Tell me," he said after a moment, "how did you do it?"

While the chair woman talked about the wheels, Victor lifted the upholstery, then let it fall to cover the wheels, over and over again. Then he said, "Where's Liv?"

A woman who had been hanging back fell into formation beside the first woman.

"Liv, I like the color," he said, "but I'm not sure about the fabric. It's a little fuzzy, or something."

"Too fuzzy?"

"I guess it's okay," Victor said. He had trouble getting himself up off the floor. The chair woman offered him a hand, but he refused it. He turned red, trying to get up on his own by doing a stomach curl, but he got caught halfway up and had to roll over onto his hands and knees to stand. His back hitched on its way up; he rubbed it with his hand and said, "Vivian! Why isn't Libby in makeup?"

An exhausted old lady in black reading glasses and a pearl necklace came around a rack of clothes and took Libby by the arm. "I've been calling her at the hotel, Vic. I left messages. Honey, we need you here at four."

"I didn't get any messages. I stay in the bungalow."

"She didn't get any messages." The woman repeated what Libby had said as though the explanation were an irresponsible excuse.

Walking with the makeup woman, Vivian, Libby said, "I usually do my own makeup."

Vivian stopped, looked at Libby for a second, then looked back over her shoulder and said, "Here, let me show you something."

She walked Libby down through a garage, past several staircases leading to nowhere, to an adjacent studio's storage space. She opened a door and said, "Behold!"

The room was piled floor to ceiling with orange chairs identical to the one on the set.

"I don't get it."

"Vic has been working on that chair for two months. That chair will be sitting to the left, in the living room, in the opening sequence. Then it will never be seen again."

"Oh my God."

"Makeup . . . is important to Vic. Appearances . . . are important when you're working with Vic."

Cynthia, Libby, and Victor were supposed to rehearse before filming, in a side room off the set. Cynthia was already there when Libby came in, five minutes early. She was in makeup, reading a novel. She put it to one side and stood.

"We've met before, in Los Angeles."

"I remember, of course. At the party with the rock garden."

"Yes." Cynthia told Libby she was honored to be working with her. She praised Libby's work. She had seen all of Libby's films, and had even seen her in a smaller production, off-Broadway, years before.

Victor came in and closed the door behind himself. He said, "Okay. Let's play the scene."

The two women played it once, and Victor looked troubled. He dug his fingers through his beard and said, "Libby, try it again. Try being really hurt."

"Hurt?"

Victor nodded, as if the direction were precise. She began the scene again. Victor slashed an arm through the air. "Stop! It's boring. Take it again from the top." She looked to Victor for direction, but he was waiting for her to begin. After an hour, when she was sure he would say he needed to rewrite the scene, he said, "Okay, let's shoot it. We have something now."

•

He sat with his back to them during takes and watched their performances on a small monitor. After all those late-night phone calls, Libby had expected him to be warm with her. She had even imagined rejecting his advances, but he spent more time giving notes to the camera operator than he spent with her.

"Let's try it again," Victor said.

Libby looked at the sound man and rolled her eyes. "I guess you can't talk about the imp."

"Stop. Let's start again from the top."

Libby mopped her face with her palms. "I guess you can't talk about the imp."

Victor swept an arm. He was huddled over his monitor in his stupid parka, with his fat back to her. He looked like a gorilla, like a gorilla in $3,000 headphones. He was showing the operator where he wanted the crosshairs to fall and when he wanted them to move. He murmured, "Like that, and then, right on 'deliberately,' I want you to get it on her cleavage. But wide, not like a tit shot."

The operator had the focus crosshairs on Cynthia's chest. "Like this?"

"Pull out. I want to see them centered, but not obvious."

Libby cleared her throat. "Victor? What do you want me to do?"

He hadn't known she was listening. He started, but recovered, and kept his back to her. "What's that?" he said.

"In the take? What should I do?"

He shrugged and craned his neck to halfway look over a heavy shoulder, so he was in profile. "Astonish me." He turned his eyes back to his monitor and said, "Let's go again."

Libby took off her coat and got it over the back of the chair. She incorporated the motion into her performance. "I guess you can't talk about the imp," she said.

"What are you talking about?" Cynthia said. "What do you mean?"

"Well, are we going to live in a portal to another dimension?"

"Stop!" Victor swept his arm. "Let's try it again."

"What am I doing wrong?" Libby asked.

"No, you're fine."

"Did you not get the tit shot right?" she spat.

Victor kept his back to her, staring into the monitor. She realized he expected her to start from the top.

"I guess you can't talk about the imp," she said.

Victor swept his arm. "Let's try it again."

The camera operator murmured something. Victor laughed. He looked at the camera operator and raised his eyebrows. The camera operator laughed.

"I guess you can't talk about the imp," Libby said.

"Wait," Victor said. "We weren't ready. Okay, let's try it again."

"I guess you can't talk about the imp."

"What are you talking about? What do you mean?" Cynthia murmured quickly. It was a simple, boring line, but Cynthia said it with venom and made it compelling.

"Well, are we going to live in a portal to another dimension?"

They went through the scene.

Victor's voice was hard. "Let's do it again. Same thing I suggested before, Libby. It's not credible, Libby."

"You never suggested *anything*," Libby said. She looked to Cynthia for support, but Cynthia was fixing her makeup. Libby turned to Victor and said, "I want suggestions. I need suggestions. I'm happy to be directed. Please tell me what you want."

Victor was quiet.

"Well, at least deign to reply."

Victor slowly took off his headphones and turned to face Libby.

She said, "Deign to answer me. I'm a human being, after all, with feelings."

Victor got up out of his chair and came over to the set. He spoke calmly. He was intent and gentle. He said, "You're the actress."

Then he looked at the scene from where he stood, turned to an assistant, and said, "Can I get a camera and monitor over here?"

They redid the scene all afternoon, into the night. After wrap, Libby and Cynthia went to a bar downtown. The bartender gave them a couple of appetizers on the house, but Libby was too nervous to eat. She drank her entire drink in a gulp and asked for another.

Cynthia said, "I have to tell you something. If you promise you can keep it a secret. I think I'm in love with Vic."

"What?"

"He made me promise not to tell anyone, especially you. But after I took the part, he started calling me all the time, sometimes several times a day, and we'd have these really intense conversations—like stuff nobody's ever asked me. You know, we'd be talking about German philosophy one minute, and then he'd be talking about beer commercials and *La Jetée*, and I know he's this short, dumpy guy with oily hair, in those beat-up trainers, but there's something so sexy about his mind, you know?"

"Sure," Libby said. "Isn't Victor married?"

"Well"—Cynthia lowered her voice—"we've been fooling around on set."

"When?"

"Only twice!" Cynthia said. "I don't want to be a home-wrecker. I totally respect the sanctity of marriage, but when Victor Vargas tells you to come into his office . . . I mean, he's irresistible, you know that. There's a reason the studios treat him like a god."

"Hm."

The two women were quiet. Libby wanted details, and she knew Cynthia wanted to give them, but to get them out of her, Libby started talking about her ex-boyfriend. When she paused, Cynthia returned to Victor.

"The first time was after your second week of shooting. He asked me to dinner, and I took a call from my agent at the table, and I could tell that really annoyed him, so he spent the meal sort of slicing Jake into fillets, saying, 'You should dump him.' And then he took me back to the studio, and he had this pack of cigarettes in his desk. I was like, 'Oh Jesus.'"

"What?"

"You don't know? I thought everybody knew."

"He smokes?"

"He's one of those guys who's *into* smoking."

Libby squinted.

"He likes you to smoke while you give him a blow job. He likes to see the cigarette by his cock."

"What!"

"I know!"

"But so did you do it?"

"Yeah, and then he was like 'You can take a shower if you want. I have to get this lighting issue worked out.'"

"Well . . ." Libby's mouth was dry. "That's okay with you?"

"The French do it. The second time, he told me to get on all fours, and I was looking at the bathroom tiles in A. With a cigarette in my mouth."

After that night she noticed the way sleeping with Victor had thrown Cynthia off balance, and the way being off balance changed her performance. She had come in a technician, but her uncertainty made her human. The shoot was supposed to wrap in three months, but Victor extended it. Five months later, Libby came in late for a rehearsal, and she was relieved to find Victor talking to the furniture people and the light people about the shine coming off the wallpaper. He was suggesting a light that the lighting guy hadn't heard of and didn't have.

He said, "I'm okay with you using what you have, as long as you can light it so we don't get that shine." He turned to Vivian and said, "What time is it? Where's Libby?"

"I'm ready to shoot," Libby said. "I'm sorry I'm late."

Victor exchanged a look with one of the technicians. "That's okay," he said. "Are you ready to go? Do you know your lines?"

"Of course."

"Really know them, Libby?"

She wasn't sure what he meant. She might have gotten into her habit of paraphrasing, but Victor hadn't complained about it. He hadn't seemed to notice.

He said, "Hey, can you hand me that," and extended his hand toward the technician, who handed him the shooting script. He turned back to Libby. "Let's go through the lines. That sounds good, for you."

Everyone was quiet, watching her.

"What?"

He laughed. "It's the first line of the scene, Libby. That sounds good, for you."

She was confused.

"Okay, Libby. Everybody, Libby's not ready. Let's— Al?"

The assistant director, a woman named Alice, stood up and came over to talk to Victor.

Libby was confused. She said, "Does anyone happen to have a breath mint or a stick of chewing gum?"

"A stick of chewing gum," Victor said. He and Al went through the door out onto the lot to confer. A few minutes later, the assistant director came back on set and said, "Victor wants to do the love scene today. Everybody clear out. Cynthia, you have the day off. Maria? Get Michael in here, into wardrobe. And Vivian? Victor wants you to dress Lib."

"Who?"

"Libby—Libby. Get her changed into the—" She gestured around her chest.

A year and a half later, back at her mother's house in Texas, Libby got a message from her agent. She said, "Good news!" and asked her to call. Libby had been nominated for an Academy Award, for best supporting actress.

"Oh."

"You don't sound excited."

"No, I am. I'm honored about it, of course."

"Is something wrong?"

"I guess I feel like Victor should have told me. I feel like since we wrapped, he's ignored me. Also, wasn't I the lead?"

"Well"—her agent always got nervous when Libby talked to her like they were friends—"I set you up with Stella McCartney. A woman there, I think it's Tiffany, is going to be in touch. Can you go in sometime this week to borrow a dress?"

Libby tried on a red floral-patterned party dress. It was mid-calf length, with a ruffled one-shoulder top. It made her look like she was forty years old and three times divorced. But she wasn't sure if that was how she looked. She walked across the floor to look in a mirror in the daylight.

"Are you shopping for a special occasion?" the clerk asked.

"I was nominated for an award," she said. "From the Academy of Arts and Letters."

"Libby Mullins, Best Supporting Actress." He laughed. He said, "I recognize you now. It didn't hit me at first. Come in back and let me show you the line."

Libby blinked.

"I mean, you're welcome to anything out here, but we have the spring line in back. I already did some pulls."

Libby was trembling. The little clerk made her nervous. He took her to his office. "That way you don't have to stand in a changing room." A few minutes later, he rolled in a rack with eleven dresses hanging on it. Libby chose four to try on, and narrowed it down to a white strapless jumpsuit.

Libby turned and looked over a shoulder at herself. "Isn't it a little 2004?"

"Not at all," the clerk said, "not for night. The sleeveless corset top makes it now. I mean, yes, it's not Oscar de la Renta pink, but who wants that for the ten thousandth time. You're unconventional."

He went away and came back with a pair of shoes. They were black patent platforms. Libby put them on. She thought she looked like Minnie Mouse.

"Aren't they a bit much?" she asked. "The contrast."

"The platform helps you." The clerk held up the right shoe. "It's an illusion." He drew a line, showing her that a three-inch heel appeared to be four-inch.

"Not the heel," Libby said. "The black against white."

"Oh." He looked disappointed. "You want to go with a silver or a skin tone?"

"I guess not."

She admired the shoes. She walked a few steps and turned. "You're shy!" he said. "I love it."

It was a beautiful day. It was sunny. On the red carpet, a few reporters stopped her. A woman asked her what it was like to work for Victor.

"Well," she said, "it was a new experience, of course."

"Are you ready to take home that award?"

"I'm certainly ready to go home."

The reporter looked confused. Libby lost her footing for a moment, and the reporter regained hers. She said, "What are you wearing?"

"The dress is someone I picked out in Stella McCartney." She corrected herself: "It's something I picked out from Stella McCartney."

"And your rings?"

"Those are all family heirlooms."

A jazz band played inside. Good and generous people wore their fine clothes. There was space, and light, and air. Libby's mother said, "It's full of magic. It's a magical evening." Libby thought about the speech she would make. If she actually won. At first she had planned to say, "Thank you," but then she had written a speech. It was on a notecard which her mother kept for her, along with extra Valium, inside her purse.

Libby said, "I'd like a glass of white wine."

People were watching her. Some openly, and some were just aware of her. She spoke to a few people she knew from other movies. Her former heroes watched her from different parts of the room. Everybody wanted a chance to speak to her. She spoke briefly to Victor. He said, "You look so pretty," in a voice that was funny, as if he were surprised. He acted like a friend, like it hadn't ever happened. Like he hadn't cut her as the lead and made her Cynthia's backup girl. Like he hadn't ignored her for almost two years.

"I've missed you," she said.

"I've missed you! This is my wife, Terry."

She shook hands with a woman who looked powerful and hard. The woman said something polite.

Libby remembered the afternoon they shot the sex scene, when Victor took her aside. After all that time craving direction . . . He had sent the crew away, and he had changed his manner completely. It was just the two of them, and Mike, on set. She'd spent so many hours in her bra and underwear she felt like she was fully dressed. He was looking at the ground, looking off into the distance, shaking his head, doing the little routine he did when he wasn't getting what he wanted out of her. It was their fourth day shooting the scene. She had been miming sucking Mike's cock for four days. He rubbed her side with his fingers.

"You had a smudge."

She shrugged.

"Do you want to put on a robe and walk with me?"

"Actually, what I'd really like is to sit down."

"Why don't you get a robe on and come to my Winnebago."

In the trailer, they sat on opposite sides of a Formica table.

He had an elaborate vacuum coffeemaker, and as he filled the bottom jug with water, he asked her why the scene wasn't working. She said she thought it was the blow job. She said that it made her uncomfortable.

"What's making you uncomfortable?" He filled the top funnel with ground coffee and put it onto the bottom jug. "It's just me and Mike. I mean, I can understand feeling uncomfortable at first, but after the initial, natural discomfort, I would think you could relax into it. I mean, *I couldn't.* But you're such a great actress."

She nodded. She watched the water boil, rise, and mix with the ground coffee. He took it off the burner and set it on the table to his right. He said, "I learned how to use one of these when I was a kid. My stepfather used them, and he always asked us to make his coffee for him. He had two children of his own, but neither of them would do it. I always did because I had these deep feelings for him, homoerotic feelings, and I thought maybe if I got his coffee right . . ."

"Hm."

"Do you know anything about stitches?"

"What?"

"I cut open my knee a few days ago, and it's—" Victor lifted the leg of his trousers. He had a gaping wound.

"Why didn't you go to the hospital immediately?"

"I hate doctors. Is it that bad?"

"Victor. Yes."

"Bad enough I should go now?"

"Well, no. I mean it's too late now."

Victor dropped his pant leg. He ran his fingers through his

beard. It was the first time he'd spoken to her this way since their phone conversations.

He said, "I've been thinking about the love scene quite a lot, and I'm concerned. It isn't a matter of discomfort. "Where is the love in this scene? Is Kate in love with her husband?"

"Not at all."

"Then why does she give him a blow job?"

"I think she's tired, and it's easier than saying no."

"Not a very good reason."

"Well," Libby shrugged.

He blew on his coffee. He sighed. He said, "Can I tell you the truth? I need you to be aroused in this scene. What would you do if I—" He stood up and crossed the Formica table to stand beside her. He put his hands on his belt buckle. He said, "What would you do if I took these off?"

Libby realized Victor's wife had said something and expected an answer. She bumbled. His wife smiled and said, "I read an article all the young girls are wearing them. So hip!"

Victor took her arm—"So nice to see you. Good luck!"—and he moved along to the next person admiring him.

Libby and her mom had thirteenth-row seats, on an aisle. But at least Victor was behind her. That meant something. He would feel that. She gave him a few glances, but he honestly didn't seem to notice.

"I need a Valium," she said.

"Are you sure? You've already had two, sweetheart."

"I need one."

Her mother palmed them to her with exaggerated caution, as though she were passing her a vial of cocaine.

At the top of the second half of the show, Libby's presenters took the podium. Libby didn't hear any of the words they said. The presenter opened the envelope and read another actress's name.

As the actress made her way up to the stage, Libby felt somebody staring at her head. She turned and saw that it was Victor. Their eyes met, and he smiled awkwardly. He waved one hand. It was an impulsive gesture. It was kind of floppy, and almost gay.

At first, Libby told people that Victor waved at her and smiled when she lost. Then she changed it a little and said he puffed an imaginary cigarette. But neither fib captured her feelings. She felt tremendously ashamed. She felt like the shame was something Victor had done to her. As the years went by, when Libby remembered the night, all she could see was the gesture that never happened.

The Imp

Lately I have been dreaming of an old woman. In the dream, the woman and I are walking. I say, "You must think I'm crazy," and the old woman says, "I don't know. If I left you, then I would have to go back to taking a different man every night."

Then the woman lowers herself down into a push-up position, and she walks on her hands and feet. We talk about her commercial success. In the dream there are mansions. The mansions are tall but thinly drawn, and the sun is near the horizon.

It is wintertime, and my calls to Kate have not been returned.

The apartment my wife and I shared for three years was on the top floor of an old stone building. Often I had trouble saying the word "wife." We had the top floor to ourselves, units

15 and 16. Sometimes in conversation, I mistakenly said girl-friend, or referred to our relationship as dating. When I said wife, it felt as though I was telling a lie.

We had two apartments, but one front door. You opened the front door, and at the end of a long entryway were two more doors, to the apartment on the left (#16) and the one on the right (#15). After some thought, we placed two bed-rooms in the unit on the left and the common areas on the right.

I was unable to sleep. Each night I fell asleep early, and then woke up and lay awake until morning. I was worried at this time about a number of things. I was growing older, my talents had been wasted, and I knew that my wife would leave me for a younger, more successful man. Also, I worried that I was losing my mind. I was having vicious thoughts. I was full of bitterness. My wife was loyal and kind—everyone who met her commented on how much she loved me—but I nursed my malevolent feelings. I mentioned this to an analyst, a man whom I met with several times. He said, "Malevolent or vicious thoughts don't necessarily imply insanity." "So she's cheating?" I said. He was openly confused by the leap. I was speaking a different language. I couldn't communicate with the analyst, and so rather than showing up for our meetings, I walked around the mall where he kept an office. I couldn't share this with my wife. In the middle of the night I sent an email to a new age couples therapist, but when she replied, I deleted the email. After sunrise I woke my wife up, gently, several times. She had trouble getting out of bed. She could only wake up when she was in danger of being late.

"You should take the car and go to the office now while you can still get there on time."

"I'll walk, so you can have the car," she murmured. She fell back asleep.

My wife was very shy. She had a moonlike face. Her features were unusually even. She was pleasant to look at, but not beautiful. When she was nervous, when she spoke to strangers, sometimes her face trembled. She was quiet for long stretches of time, and believed in silly things.

After she was gone, I stayed in bed and did nothing. I was tired, and then I was frustrated, and after some time I opened my wife's computer and turned on Outlook Express. I read her incoming mail. It was mostly communications with coworkers about small matters. I read what she had sent. Her replies were short, cordial, and efficient. I couldn't find any secrets. I typed the name of her last boyfriend into her sent-mail box and read her emails to him. Then I went online and typed in the name of my last girlfriend and looked at photographs of her.

My first marriage ended when I'd had an affair. So I know how quickly these things happen. The wind blows, and a five-year commitment falls apart.

I went back to my wife's inbox, and I found a love letter that she had written when she was in her twenties, to one of her old flames. She described a trip to the farmers' market, dresses she wanted to buy, and the color of some berries that she had bought. The berries were green. It was not what she said, it was the way she said it.

I got out of bed, went to the kitchen, and ate a handful of Brazil nuts. I stood in front of the sink. I can say these things now. At the time I couldn't even think them to myself in an honest way.

In the car, I turned on Siri and said, "Driving directions. Trader Joe's, Palo Alto." Siri said, "I don't understand." I said it again, four or five times. My wife worked for a company that designed operating systems. I told her she should work on problems like this. "Everyday things. Then you'd make us rich."

"You'll make us rich with the new play," she said, and then she corrected herself. "The new production. Besides, I am happy in our life. We have everything we need."

Siri called out directions, and I followed them. I managed to get lost. I have a poor sense of direction. I always miss exits at the worst time. This happened and I had to drive ten miles on an open stretch before I could turn around.

The phone rang and I put it on speakerphone. It was my father. He said, "Did you drive by the place I sent? I saw you opened the photos."

"No."

"Why won't you look in the Redwoods? They have nice things there. You could easily find something."

I was driving on the highway and trying to figure out how to pull up directions on a different program. My father said, "Tom?"

"Don't use my name like that."

"Like what?"

"Don't use it when you're angry. You know like what, you're not stupid. Besides, the fog is dangerous."

"What?"

"The fog is dangerous in the Redwoods."

"It's not so bad. I drove through it at night."

"You shouldn't have done that."

"But people do live there, don't they?"

"They don't commute. I can't have this discussion."

"I guess you can't talk about the sleep clinic."

"I'm lost on the freeway. I don't want to discuss checking myself into a new age asylum."

"Well, are you going to just— Tom, you're under strain. I'm worried about you. You can't live in that drafty old apartment. I couldn't sleep there either, and frankly, if you stay there, you'll lose Kate. I think your marriage should be your first priority."

"Boundaries." I hung up the phone. I took an exit and pulled into the gas station to buy a pack of cigarettes.

In the parking lot of the grocery store half an hour later, I called my father and apologized. My father said, "Son, it is not your fault. You're not sleeping. I wish you all would at least come out to the house."

"We'll try."

My father had struggled with psychiatric problems, and so had my mom.

It's true I was very tired. Standing in front of one particular segment of floor cleaners, I picked up a scouring sponge and a package of sponges with dual sides. I didn't know how I was supposed to decide between them.

At dinner, my wife talked about semaphores, possible synchronization problems, and her junior staff. I often felt worn down when she spoke. I felt frustrated, then nauseated. I realized that I would be sick and ran to the kitchen sink, where I threw up. I put my hands above my head and grasped the cabinet pulls and vomited. Then I turned and put a hand to my throat—I couldn't get any air. I turned back to the sink and threw up.

When I came back to the table, my wife took her plate to the kitchen. She was trying to be polite, but she was confused.

"Are you sick?" she asked.

"Isn't it obvious?"

"Maybe you should lie down."

"I'm not sick. I'm revolted. By you. All this talk about your office. Just to rub my nose in it. Why don't you just say I'm a failure?"

"Ordinarily you like to hear how I describe things," she said. "I think you're unhappy."

"Is that a joke?"

"What?"

"Jesus fucking Christ."

I stood up and walked out of the room. I left my plate on the table. I went to the other side of the apartment. With the lights out, I got into pajamas and went to bed. I heard her go to the kitchen and run water to scrub the sink and wash my dish.

My wife is very particular about being clean. When I first met her parents, and she left the room, her father leaned in and said, "Let me warn you, my daughter is a bit obsessive about hygiene. I once caught her washing the sugar."

"Really," I said.

"That is not a joke."

Later I asked my wife if she washed the sugar, and she said, "That's ridiculous. How could I wash sugar."

In bed, I thought about how a few nights before, my wife had gone to eat ice cream. She was on the other side of the apartment a long time. Her phone must have been hidden over there, on the other side of the apartment, so she could write in secret about the color of berries, and things like that, to other men—men from her office, the man who had come to repair the sink. I thought of the places where the phone might have been stowed, and the things they could get up to with just two smartphones. Then I thought of her in her office, and all the possibilities there, and I wondered about setting her phone to "find my phone" so that I could remotely follow her, but I could never do that. Then I planned what I would do the next morning after she left the apartment, how I would go into her email and search for things. But then, I realized, she would have a secret account. When my wife got into bed, she said, "I think I am pregnant."

"I'm sleeping."

"What?" She shook my arm. "Tom?"

"Just let me be weird awhile."

She said again she was pregnant—she had missed two periods. My ex-wife is often telling me that my wife and I should not have a child. She says that her psychologist advised it. I lay there angry about that—how dare my ex-wife get involved in such a way. Really, it was outrageous. She was addicted to Adderall, an attorney who was literally paid in wasps' nests.

"Don't you have anything to say?" my wife said.

"Just ignore me," I said. I was picturing my ex-wife in her psychologist's office. It made me very angry.

"If you want to be ignored, then say, 'I'm getting tired, I'm going to sleep.' Don't get up and storm out. I said I think I'm pregnant. What the hell is your problem? Snap out of it. Stop feeling so sorry for yourself. I'm pregnant. You need to talk to me."

She realized how mad she was as she spoke. She started to curse, to list my character flaws. When she talks like that, I can't quite hear it. My adrenaline must shoot up too high. So I can't remember what she said. She cursed and threw my glasses. They didn't break. My wife was funny that way. She threw things, but they would never break.

I got out of bed and went to the other side of the apartment. I could not bear to say that I was jealous, that I was all alone, that I spent my life engrossed in imaginary conspiracies and humiliations, that we were haunted.

The next afternoon, while my wife was away, the phone rang.

"It's Gwen from the Stokes Institute returning your call."

"The Stokes what?"

"You called me. You're having some difficulties in your marriage."

"Oh yes, that was just crazy."

She laughed. She said she could do a remote reading at no charge.

"Do you have some kind of electronic device?"

"Just my tarot cards."

"I don't believe in tarot cards. Think about how that sounds to me. You can help me with my marriage over the phone with your cards? Think about it. I didn't realize you were like this."

"The cards help me. I have fixed ideas. The cards help me see it differently, with an open mind."

"I don't believe in nonsense."

"It's free."

"Look, I don't give a damn how you think about it. One day I looked at my hands and they were smeared with shit."

"A common sign of psychological disturbance."

"But the shit wasn't mine."

"The mind manifests that, honey. It can manifest anything. Flash openness, and I'm going to lay out the cards. Just be quiet."

I said, "My wife is pregnant."

"Yeah, this is just your reading. The little being, she's . . . if she was human it was a long time ago. She's not malevolent, but she's very negative."

I laughed, "So this is like a devil? My baby?"

"I didn't do a reading for your wife or for your unborn

child. I'm talking about this being that is obsessed with you. There is a ghost on you."

I felt a cold fear. I also felt similar to how I had felt in school, the time I had lice. I knew she was right, and that I should ask her how to proceed. But another part of me overrode those feelings. The woman was a crazy con artist, or a flake.

Still, I said, "Hypothetically, if one spouse were cheating on the other, could your cards see it?"

"Your wife isn't cheating."

"Did you lay out the cards?"

For the short term, she advised me to bathe a lot. She said it was important to get a cleaning. She said she would do it for me. I said to go ahead, and she explained it had to be done in person, as soon as possible. "How much?" I asked. She quoted a price in four figures. She wasn't available to come to our apartment. She said, "You can come to the center. You'll have to stay a couple nights."

A sign in front of Gwen's house said THE STOKES INSTITUTE.

"It looks like it was the show house for the development," my wife said. "I'm surprised they let her put that sign up."

"If you're going to be like this, we may as well turn around."

"What? What did I say?"

"I've been very honest with you . . ."

Gwen came to the door in a purple sweatshirt and sweatpants bunched up to her knees. She was about sixty-five years old, with pin-straight blond hair that reached her shoulders, and perfectly cut bangs. She had a smooth brow and round, gentle eyes. She was very thin and walked with her hips tilted forward. I started to introduce myself and she cut me off. "I know." She introduced herself to my wife and offered us tea. She took us on a tour, starting with the sewing room, and then each of the four bedrooms. She showed us the bathroom and pointed out the small tub. She went back to her enormous kitchen with skylights showing the fog and glass patio doors to more fog rolling outside. Then she said, "Let me show you my work space." On the walls were photographs of Gwen in her twenties. She had been remarkably beautiful.

"That looks like a Helmut Newton," my wife said.

"It is," Gwen said. "I used to be somewhat attractive."

"Somewhat," I joked. She ignored me. I could tell that Gwen's past changed my wife's impression of her.

We went into a garden room that was made almost entirely of glass and had a shining wooden floor. There was a kind of shrine, like a series of stacking tables, each in a different kind of natural stone. They had crystals jutting from their sides so they looked like slices of rock from a rock-and-gem show. On each surface were golden bowls full of water, or flowers, or cake. One held a mirror and a painting of a lady.

"Each stone has its own power," Gwen started to explain. "That first layer is pure amethyst. After that is agate—"

My wife said she needed to use the restroom. She asked me to come in with her. She closed the bathroom door, sat on the toilet. She rested her head in her hands. "We have to drive home through all this fog."

"No, don't worry. Gwen said we can stay a couple of nights—actually, we need to for the purification."

She moaned. She said, "How did this happen? How did I wind up in this position?"

She got a Valium out of her purse.

"Can I have one?" I said.

She took it out of her mouth, split it, and gave me half. In moments like this I saw my wife correctly. She said, "What are we going to eat?"

"I'll go and ask."

I was halfway down the stairs when I stopped. I put my hand on the wall to catch my breath. All of the grievances and burdens of my life overwhelmed me, and I went upstairs and apologized to my wife. I said, "I couldn't ask."

"Well, if we're staying here, we're staying here," she said. "Let's just go downstairs, tell her we're tired, and ask her where we're sleeping."

My wife and I got in bed and held each other. She said, "Scratch my back."

I put a hand through the sleeve of her T-shirt.

"No, higher. Higher. There, now over to the middle."

I scratched with both hands.

"Hey, there's a wolverine," she said. "Ow."

"There's a wolverine?" I stopped scratching and looked at my nails.

"Yeah."

"Where?" I held out my left hand.

She touched each of my fingers with her tongue. She said, "I don't know. I can't find it now."

I looked at my pinkie. "I think it's this one."

"Maybe so, I didn't check that one."

I bit the nail down and said, "Turn over." I scratched her back again.

She said, "Ow, it's still there. The wolverine."

"I had it lifted!" I said.

She turned over and I held up my hand to show her that the pinkie was curled up.

There was a knock at the bedroom door.

"Come in," I said. "Come in." I said it a few times. Then I got up and opened the door. I didn't even bother putting on a shirt. Gwen didn't seem to notice.

"I'm going to the store," she said.

"We were just going to sleep."

"Isn't your wife hungry?"

I turned. My wife shrugged.

"Let me go," Gwen said. "I don't mind. She's got to eat for two, right? I'll get some materials for a purification while I'm gone."

"You told her I'm pregnant?" my wife asked.

I got back in bed beside her. We were both in our underwear. I said, "Let's cuddle until she gets back. Enfold me in your wax wing."

She chuckled. I turned my back to her and she put an arm around me.

Gwen was gone for an hour. She came back with takeout: steaks, gumbo, and arugula salad. It was too much food for

me—too rich and too late, but my wife ate everything. I was
ready to go to bed, but Gwen lit a fire. She read a prayer, and
burned food. I kept looking at my wife, to say, "Where are
we, this is crazy?" but my wife was watching Gwen intently.
Gwen said, "I am offering everything nice in the world to the
being—whatever she would like. I'm asking her to go."

"What being?" my wife asked.

"There's a ghost living on me," I told my wife. "Gwen
said so."

Gwen said, "Don't pin it all on me."

My wife said, "Actually, right now, that makes a lot of sense."

When Gwen was finished, we all felt better. I felt better
because I could go to sleep, and my wife felt better because she
hoped something would change me back to the man I used
to be. Gwen said, "The being is still there. She is happy now,
but she is strong."

As we were falling asleep, my wife said, "Why don't we
just live here?"

"In Gwen's house?"

"No, in a house like it. In the Redwoods."

The next afternoon Gwen sent my wife and me to the Kroger's
near the house to get materials for the next ritual, what she
called the real purification. I coughed several times each block.
My wife said, "Could you not make that last sound?"

"It hurts."

"I know. Just that last sound."

"It hurts me."

"It feels very aggressive."

I rolled down my window and leaned against my elbow. I coughed more, and hacked. I coughed in the grocery store. People turned to watch, so I did it louder to show them it was up to me whether I coughed. I even considered spitting in the aisle, to show them. The grocery store was much bigger than the kind of grocery store I was accustomed to, but the food was not arranged well at all. My wife said she would get the ritual materials from Gwen's list. She told me to get food. I was too disoriented to shop. I put ice cream and salt-and-vinegar potato chips into my basket. When my wife found me, she looked at the two items and then at me. I was angry. I didn't know why I was angry, so I coughed. I said, "We can always come back."

At the checkout register my wife said, "What about Gwen? She's hosting us. I bet she'd like a burger."

"I don't think so. She strikes me as a vegetarian."

My wife gave me a funny look I didn't understand. I understand it now. It was very simple, of course. My wife was hungry. My wife would have liked a burger.

Gwen performed the big purification when we got home. It took her several hours to prepare. She had to cook an elaborate meal, and she took some time in her bedroom getting dressed in an organza robe and a crown. By this time, I had hope. Maybe, I thought, maybe it will all work out. Maybe it's true what she says—hadn't I been acting strangely? Wasn't jealousy another word for possession? She lit a fire outside and read a long text. The fog lifted during the ceremony—due to the sun, I thought, but Gwen said it was auspicious.

"I'm cured?" I said.

"I don't know. The being is a bit more powerful than ordinary. If it were me, I would not ever set foot again in your apartment."

We would stay a second night. She wanted to call another expert. She warned me that the being had her feelings hurt and might get up to mischief.

That night, my wife and I got a DVD from Gwen's collection. We chose *No Country for Old Men*. We were both exhausted. During one of the first scenes, Chigur was handcuffed behind his back. He slipped the handcuffs down his legs and stepped over them, so he could have his arms in front. My wife said, "Why don't people do that more often?"

"They do. I did it every time I went to jail. It's just they fuss at you."

"They fuss at you how?"

"They say, 'What the hell do you think you're doing?'"

I was too tired to stay up. I said, "I think I'm going to sleep."

When I woke up, my wife was sitting cross-legged on the floor. She was in the corner with her phone and the movie had started to replay.

"Who are you texting?" I said.

"My mother."

"Why is the movie starting over again?"

"I wanted to see something I missed the first time."

"Why are you on the floor?"

"I was eating pretzels."

"Let me see the texts."

She sighed. She stood and handed me the phone. There were two or three recent texts between her and her mother. A text message rolled in from a phone number. I recognized the number. It was an old boyfriend of hers. I felt sick, like I would faint. I didn't read what it said. I threw the phone across the room.

"You were texting an old boyfriend."

"I was texting my mother."

She got the phone from the other side of the room. I tried to take it, but she held it behind her back. I knocked her onto the floor. It happened quickly.

"Show it to me," I said. "I don't care if you like him. I want you to go and be with him. You two are a very good match, in my opinion."

I hit her in the face. She said, "Hit me one more time."

I said, "Show it to me."

"No. I won't put up with this tyranny anymore."

I stomped my wife's foot and knocked her over. She tried to fight me. I took her hands and hit myself in the face.

I said, "Why, if you were going to do this, did you marry me? I was perfectly happy to be alone."

"You're crazy."

"I saw the number."

She gave me the phone and said, "So call it. Go ahead."

I went to the bathroom. I locked the door. I thought she

might come in, and so I got into the tub. I clicked the number, and after a few rings, a man answered. He said, "Hello?" I saw a plastic razor and imagined taking it out, how I would like to rake it across my wrist, or her face, and then for just a moment I saw the imp. She was dirty and slimy like something that had been in the drain for decades. She was made of hair and slime. She had her hands around my throat. But I must have been hallucinating, right?

When I came out of the bathroom, my wife was on the floor. I kneeled and lifted her head. I took her into my lap. She was my only friend in this world.

The Sew Man

Particularly at a certain time in my life, I looked at a suit and imagined myself in it, talking to a woman. I am a passionate person. I was in Kashmir in wintertime, and I was the only guest at Butt's Clairmont Estate. Every afternoon the hotel owner, Mr. Butt, came into my houseboat, sat down, ran his hands over the knees of his trousers, and tried to make conversation. One day I complimented his jacket—he always dressed elegantly—and he said, "Do you like suits, Mr. Nudell? You can meet my tailor."

The tailor had a corner storefront with a receiving area and a fitting room. In the fitting room, one wall was covered by a sheet, and three had built-in shelves that ran floor to ceiling and were stacked with bolts of fabric. On the top of a pile of folded remnants close to the ceiling was a piece of yellow fabric. It looked like velvet. I stood on a chair and pulled it down.

"What is it?" I said.

"Sir, we call this corduroy."

Mr. K. Salama wore a burgundy turtleneck, a white collared shirt, and a tweed jacket. His assistant was short and thin, and he stood in the corner. Salama talked. His voice was deep and rich, and he talked in a stream. Only one word stood out: suit. When Salama said suit, something strange happened.

"You might like to have made a suit, sir," he said. "I can make you a very nice suit for a reasonable price."

I had brought a collared shirt. "I came to have this shirt copied," I said.

Salama lifted the shirt and let it fall. "Lot of gentlemen like to have a suit made. I can make you a very nice suit, with a jacket and pants, and that can be a very good thing to have."

He picked up a catalog, flipped past pictures of old men in high-waisted underwear, and stopped at a photo. He turned the catalog to show me a middle-aged man in a suit. The man in the picture looked like he sold shoes at a department store. Salama gauged my reaction and paged through the catalog some more. He stopped, and showed me a picture of a man who looked like John Goodman. I shrugged.

He said, "Lot of gentlemen like to have a two-button jacket made. For travel, that can be a very good thing to have." He turned the catalog and showed me a wool jacket. It was gray and fit the young model nicely. I said, "Hmm."

Salama snapped, and the smaller man jumped and left the room.

"For travel, that can be a very nice thing to have. What day are you leaving?"

"Friday."

"Well, it's no problem, if you don't want to carry it, we can mail it to your home. You can even pay me when you get home, we have done that before in the past and it always works very well."

Still talking—always talking—he went to a wall and lifted a sheet. Behind it was another built-in shelf, piled with bolts of gray wool. The small man returned with a pitcher of green tea and a basket of fresh biscuits, cake, and macaroons. Salama sat on the floor. "Please eat the cake," he said. He took several produce bags full of fabric swatches out of a shopping bag. He dumped the wool swatches onto the carpet.

"This one I can make it you. I can give you a very good price."

He held up a lightweight gray wool. I took it from him and looked at it closely.

"Is it wool?"

"Sir, this is wool."

"A hundred percent?" I said. "It's a hundred percent wool?"

"One hundred percent. No additions."

"Yes," I said, "this one would be all right."

He stood, flipped back the sheet again, and withdrew a bolt of gray wool. Taking the rolled fabric by its cut end, he flipped the bolt onto the floor and draped the unfurled fabric over an extended arm.

"Is that the same as this one?" I held up the swatch to compare. The swatch was a perfect gray. The bolt was a somber charcoal.

He unrolled a second gray wool, a third, and a fourth. He talked the whole time. He told me about his first suit, which had been paid for by his parents, as he unrolled the eighth. It was lovat, he said, four buttons. He described it in detail. He said he had the sleeves and legs taken in. He flipped open the twelfth bolt, and then I realized he didn't have the gray I wanted, and he had made a mess in his studio, and I was going to leave without buying anything.

"It's getting late," I said.

"You want a suit. How about an overcoat? Like this one." He went to a closet and struggled with the zipper on a bag.

"I have an overcoat."

I pointed to the coat I was wearing, and he made a face. He said something to the little man, who brought out a binder full of testimonials. Salama paged through them and pointed to the wall, at two framed letters. Before I could go read them, Salama pointed to a handwritten letter in the binder. It included a picture of a broad-hipped, sallow, middle-aged woman in a charcoal skirt suit. In her letter, she mentioned having worn her suit for a television interview ("There's some exposure for you") and said she was sorry she had not been able to mention Salama by name. He flipped past that letter to a typewritten one on yellowing paper. It was written by a British official, and it didn't mention the suit. The official just said that Salama had not cheated him.

"Have more cake," Salama said. He brought out a navy blazer and explained he had made it for someone from the embassy. It had brass buttons. I wondered why the ambassador hadn't taken the jacket. I said, "Nice buttons." He began to measure me. I pointed to a fabric. Then I pointed to something else. Soon I was the future owner of a brown wool suit, a salmon cashmere blazer, and four collared shirts.

"Now I know your taste," Salama said. He brought down a bolt of white velvet. "How about I make it you a suit. Cotton velvet, sir. How about we make it a suit. Slim pants and jacket, I can make it you. I want to be your family tailor."

I nodded once.

"How about a little deposit, something for a little luck?"

He rubbed two fingers together, and I slipped 2,000 rupees into his hand. It was a small deposit, but neither of us, in that moment, was afraid of anything.

"The sew man hasn't yet come with your suit," Salama said.

He rang a bell, and the little assistant came and stood in the doorway. Salama sent him out for tea. I sat and paged through a catalog until the little man came back. This time he brought green tea, macaroons, and a hot dog wiener. I drank my tea for a while. Salama went away and came back. Then I felt someone behind me and turned to see a man in his forties. He had strange eyes that did not give or receive light. Salama said, "Sir, please meet my son."

"How do you like Kashmir?" Salama's son asked.

"I like it very much."

"Welcome. Most welcome."

When the tailor of my suit—the sew man—came in through a side door, he walked fast, bent forward at the waist, like someone who is afraid of being beaten. He was trembling with excitement and fear. He wore his baggy trousers rolled up all the way to his mid-calf and carried the brown suit, removing it from its hanger as he apologized to Salama.

"But you must come in summer," Salama's son said. "Then everything is in flower."

Salama took the pants from the sew man, expressing some annoyance at the wait and at the sew man's anxiety. With great calm he brought the pants to me. "The pants, sir!"

"Have you been to Gulmarg?" his son asked.

"Please try them on, sir," Salama said, and the three men watched me do it. All this time Salama's son was talking, and it occurred to me that he was used to being ignored.

The trousers were loose. They had wide legs and the waist hung. Salama brought out the blazer. It had white circles of muslin for buttons, and no form to its collar. I put it on. It was loose in the shoulders and reached my mid-thighs. The lapels were wide. I had somehow turned old. I looked unbearably old.

"This isn't what I had in mind." I took off the jacket. My plan was to go and never come back. I said, "Maybe I should go and we can work this out some other time."

Salama picked up his catalog. "Sir, you have asked me to make this for you and I have made it."

He pointed to John Goodman.

"That's the wrong picture!" I said. "That isn't the suit."

I tore off the blazer, dropped it onto the floor, pulled the door open, and left.

After breakfast I watched the fishermen. They sat on the noses of flat-bottomed boats about half the size of a kayak, with their legs tucked under their wool shirts. It looked familiar.

When they cast their nets, it looked like they were tossing mud or vomiting. And they did something mysterious with sticks. They'd sit still for fifteen minutes watching the water, then, with one measured stroke after another, they thrust their poles into the water.

Ramzana, the man who brought me my food every day, opened the sliding door to my houseboat.

"The tailor is here for you."

Salama took off his mittens and put them on my desk. He unwound his scarf and draped it over the back of a chair. He got down onto his knees and began to rummage through a canvas tote bag. "I did not see you yesterday, so I came after prayers."

He withdrew the salmon jacket I'd ordered and unfolded it. Still kneeling, he held it out to me. I got up out of my chair and I put it on. I went in back, to the bathroom, to look at myself.

In the blazer I looked like my dad. I looked yellow, and I looked very old. I tried pulling at the lapels, buttoning and unbuttoning the coat, and looking at different angles, but the coat was awful. I came back out, nodded, and said, "It's good."

"Sir"—he draped the coat over a chair back—"if you don't mind, how much deposit had you left."

"Two thousand rupees."

"Sir, if it's not any trouble . . ."

I began counting out more money. "How much is that jacket?"

"Just forty-eight hundred."

"I'll just pay you for it now," I said, and counted out $34.

Salama's scraping and bowing had an effect on me. I was being rude to him the way my rich friends had been rude to me, and the way salespeople at Neiman Marcus had been rude to my father. I was acting as though it was simple. If I spent my whole life like that, as the one with the money, I'd probably say things like "There's no need for the hand-wringing, Mr. Salama." It was funny how fast it happened.

Salama took the catalog out of his sack and paged through it until he found my measurements. "Sir, if you like, we can go ahead and make you the white suit as you have said."

"No," I said. "No."

Mournfully, Salama turned to the chair back over which he had draped his scarf. He picked up his scarf slowly and wound it about his neck. He took his mittens in hand—they were oversize, and hand-knit, like Mickey Mouse gloves. He put them on, then took them off and put them back on the desk. He coughed. He switched his bag from one arm to the other, bent over, and somehow the salmon blazer slid off the chair back and caught his jacket. One of its loose strings looped itself around one of his suit-coat buttons, and he let it hang there. He bent over, rummaging through his sacks, and my blazer hung from him. He knew the effect he was having. He withdrew two plastic grocery sacks from his tote. Then, in unhurried silence, he detached the blazer from his button and replaced it over the chair back. He withdrew a circle of European-style puff pastry from one of the bags and started to heat it by holding it just above my steel, wood-burning oven.

"Sir, would you like to taste?"

"I just ate."

"It is from the mountains."

"Thank you. I'm sorry—I just ate."

He put it on my saucer.

"Business," he said, "is very bad."

His eyes misted over, reddened, and became impenetrable. His son, he explained, his leg—the medicine—because of the tango. Something else; then, "The suit."

"All right," I said. "Make me the suit."

His eyes cleared. He became light. He efficiently put his things around himself and was out. A minute passed, and I stood and opened the houseboat door. Salama was there on my porch. He was smoking.

"Sir, you smoke? You like to have a cigarette?"

Salama was still there when I was dressed to leave for town. I had to go to the Kingfisher office in Srinagar to buy tickets to New Delhi. I had decided to leave Kashmir. Salama was leaning against the opened door of my car, talking to my driver. When I got into the front seat, Salama slid into the back and leaned forward.

"Sir, it is okay I ride with you? Just to the city."

Finally I was angry. My driver had three teeth. He held his mouth open. When it started to rain, we had to roll up the windows, and then I could smell his breath. I haven't ever smelled anything as bad as that. We drove for an hour. Salama sat in the backseat smoking and complaining.

"These roads are awful," he said. "Just mud. The country has gone to pot since the British left. Everything has gone to ruin. Indians can't run things. Have you seen an Indian bathroom, sir? And the workers who defecate in the street."

When Mr. Butt came to my room that afternoon, I told him I was going to be leaving early. I blamed the tailor—it was all so minor—and I started to cry. It seemed okay to me, because Mr. Butt had cried in front of me several times by then, but he was uncomfortable and confused. He said, "If you don't want the suits, just tell him you don't want them, he made you the wrong one."

"I don't want the suits. But how can I say that? I ordered them."

"He did make you the wrong one?"

"I don't know. Please, make him leave me alone."

Mr. Butt looked around anxiously. Then he cried. He wiped his tears and said, "He is not my usual tailor."

We cried together for a little while. Then Mr. Butt said, "Come to dinner at my house."

Mr. Butt's house was perfectly elegant—the sort of elegance one rarely sees anywhere, and while I had known Mr. Butt was wealthy like this, the house surprised me. It reminded me of the house in *Fanny and Alexander*—it had that kind of charm touched by family magic.

In the family room, Mr. Butt's wife lay bedridden, with a feeding tube in her nose. Her hand was taken from between the sheets and placed into mine. I realized that I was expected to talk to her.

I said, "I'm staying at the houseboats."

She said something and I leaned forward.

"She doesn't speak English," Mr. Butt said.

"What did she say?"

"We can't understand her."

"I'm here until tomorrow," I said. "The houseboats are very nice. Thank you. I've enjoyed my time as a guest." I held her hand a little longer.

Mr. Butt and I sat on the floor, leaned against pillows. One of his servants left the room and returned with Salama and a fierce-looking young woman in a T-shirt, sneakers, and jeans. Salama began to lay out clothes—the brown suit, the shirts, and the white suit.

"Sir, you see, we have been working many hours."

"The shirts are fine," I said. "I don't want the suit."

Mr. Butt winced.

"Please, sir." Salama held out the white suit. "I have made it you. Please try."

The young woman looked into my eyes. "You have ordered this suit, and my father has made it you." She was trying to bully me, but her heart wasn't in it.

I took the suit from Mr. Salama. One of Butt's sons took me to a bedroom where I could change. I noticed a plate tipped against an old-fashioned, high-end hi-fi. He saw me looking and took a long time explaining where it had come from. For him the plate had magic.

The suit was the kind I had often seen on other men. It fit me. It drew me together. I felt different inside it. Young. I wanted to stay alone in the room, in the suit, but I would have to come out.

Servants brought a cloth, bowls, rice, several dishes. Silverware and china were brought for me. Salama and his daughter sat cross-legged and ate off silver plates, using their hands. Mr. Butt ate out of a silver trophy. He sat on his knees, with his shoulders stooped. He stared at the floor and put one and then another fistful of food into his mouth.

After we had eaten, Mr. Salama said, "Now, if it is all right, you could walk for us."

I walked around Mr. Butt's living room, back and forth in front of the cot and his wife, Salama and his daughter, until they were satisfied. Then I sat cross-legged in my exquisite suit, and we drank tea. This is the way it is for me. This is the way it is for the people I love. My dad had a plastic basin in his closet full of $600 shoes, but he wore Tiddies—those rubber-soled flip-flops—and had his hair cut at a gay men's salon. We are people who never get it right.

Frank Advice for Fat Women

A woman who was lonely and depressed should begin by getting on some medication. She should clean her house and throw away clutter. After that, Dr. Sheppard told his patients to lose weight and wear dresses.

He and his wife had shared a practice for twenty years, and so they had—after some initial attempts to carry on as usual—made a short-term arrangement: he saw his patients in the mornings, and Isabel saw hers in the afternoons. She would not speak to him. Together they had agreed on a clean break.

His new academic appointment filled the downtime. He kept to his schedule. He meditated in the mornings, jogged three afternoons a week. When he noticed an uptick in his night eating, he hired a nutritionist. He was eating better than he had in years.

Then Catherine Summer called. His secretary told him that Mrs. Summer had been referred by Columbia's dean and wanted to see him, or something. "She has anxiety." When Dr. Sheppard finally spoke with Mrs. Summer on the telephone, she explained that her daughter had suffered a panic attack at Morts Restaurant in St. Louis.

"Debbie's been in New York five years. She hasn't done anything. She interned at *Town & Country* and she volunteered at the Morgan, but from what I can gather, all she does is eat and drink. We pay her expenses—we always have—but of course that is with the expectation that *eventually* she will find her way. Now it seems like she's developing these disorders."

"I'm sorry to say I've recently accepted a position at Columbia University, in addition to my private practice, so as you can imagine—"

"How nice. Debbie's almost twenty-eight years old, and she has no plans for a career, no boyfriend. Dr. Angel said you were the right one for us."

"Oh, you know Don? That's interesting, Mrs. Summer. You'll have to tell him I said hello."

"Debbie didn't use to have a weight problem, or any problem, but her last boyfriend was overweight, and some of his eating habits rubbed off on her. Over Christmas she'd sit in front of the television with a sleeve of crackers and a block of cheese, and I'd say, 'Go out! Do something!' I know she could lose the weight easily, if she'd simply *do* something, but she won't listen to my suggestions, and I'm worried, with her father's metabolism, if she lets herself reach thirty without losing the weight, it'll just stay on her. After a certain age, a woman's body just won't respond to diet or exercise—our estrogen levels change—and of course there are procedures, but *why* go down that road? She's just a girl! Of course I'm happy to pay for liposuction if she'll take it, but I tell her it's simple: don't eat. All the diet gurus in the world are peddling the same line of bullshit, excuse me, but if you want to lose weight, stop eating."

Dr. Sheppard looked at the nineteenth-century Satsuma vase on the corner of his desk. It was one of two, about the size of a lamp, and had been commissioned for a Russian general, to resemble a lighthouse. It had been a gift from Isabel's mother to the couple when they married.

"Hello? Dr. Sheppard? The sooner the better, honestly. We need your help. I'm asking as a mother."

"Yes, sorry, I'm here." He asked if Debbie would be free to meet at lunchtime.

"Of course—she doesn't have a job. I believe I mentioned that."

He began to take notes.

Debbie threw herself into the armchair opposite his desk. His first impression was that she was remarkably pretty. Her hair was almost blond, and it was long and straight. She dressed mannishly—in jeans, a wool crewneck sweater, a worn-out blue oxford shirt, and high-quality, unpolished loafers—but she couldn't hide her looks. Her diamond earrings caught his eye throughout the conversation.

Debbie *was* slightly overweight, and her posture was bad, but her manners were good. She looked Dr. Sheppard directly in the eye when she said, "Thank you for meeting me. My mother told me you made an exception for her. She's very happy that I'm here."

"How do you feel about it?"

"I'm doing my best to humor everybody."

"What do you mean?"

"I mean my mom wants me here, and so fuck it. No offense."

Dr. Sheppard nodded. He glanced over the intake questionnaire. No health problems, no smoking, no problems with alcohol. Asked to list her number of drinks, Debbie checked the box "four–five a night." So, a problem with alcohol. She didn't exercise. She slept between ten and twelve hours nightly. In answer to the question "Why did you come in today?" she wrote, "I'd like to find a solution to life's mysteries."

"What about, do you have anxiety? Your mother mentioned something at Morts."

Debbie pressed her face into her hands and took a deep breath. "I had a panic attach, okay? I think they're pretty normal. My mom acts like I have a gnome or something."

"A what?"

"Ugh, a movie I saw. This schizo guy had a gnome that made him drink rye."

Dr. Sheppard didn't press her, but he made a note. Of course she had intended to say panic attack, but the word she spoke was "attach." He prescribed a low daily dose of Prozac, Ativan as needed for mild anxiety, and a monthly supply of ten four-milligram Xanax for severe panic. He asked Debbie to come back two days later, on Thursday, and to see him twice weekly until they were comfortable with each other. As she was leaving with the papers, he said, "Do you feel all right about that? How do you feel?"

"Compromised," Debbie said. "See you Thursday."

He was in his school office eating a Potbelly sandwich later that afternoon—he taught Tuesdays from 4:30 to 6:20—when Mrs. Summer called and asked if he had a moment to chat.

"Well, to be honest, Mrs. Summer, I teach in a few minutes."

"It's Kitty."

"I generally take this time to prepare."

"Well, this won't take any time at all. I'm calling to ask a favor. I understand things went well with Debbie, and I want to thank you, by the way. But the reason for my call is, my husband and I are in Stockholm just now and I wanted to have his secretary send you a check. So, just your best mailing address."

"Sure." He gave his address at the office. Then he couldn't help showing off. He said, "As it happens, I'll be in Stockholm next month for an IHS meeting. I'll be speaking. How's the weather? Should I bring a coat?"

"Oh, hooray! We can meet. Debbie said you were wonderful, but I don't think you really know a person until you spend some time one-on-one."

"Well, that's nice to hear—about Debbie. My impression was that Debbie was feeling ambivalent about her treatment."

"Ah," she said. "I'm sorry to run on you, that's my other line."

The IHS meeting was held at a modern conference hotel out-side Stockholm. The lobby was full of excited young doctors and pharmaceutical representatives, many of whom already wore their lanyard badges.

Dr. Sheppard made it through the lobby with a few hand-shakes. He had submitted a paper for presentation, but it had been accepted for the congress. What that meant was that he was not asked to speak before five hundred colleagues but to compress his research to fit a poster, which he would hang among a thousand others and present to a panel of three eval-uators. Ordinarily, researchers of his stature responded to con-gress selection by sending a nurse or a research assistant to the meeting.

The congress looked like a high school science fair. Cloth panels with pushpins in their upper-left-hand corners snaked through the room, and youngsters nervously hung their work. Dr. Sheppard had trouble hanging his poster. He struggled with it.

"Need some help?"

He looked up at the woman who had her hand on his poster.

"Kitty. Kitty Summer. In the flesh. I'm so pleased to meet you, Dr. Sheppard."

Mrs. Summer was more attractive than her daughter. She was greyhound-thin, and she wore patent heels, a slim-waisted skirt suit, and a short string of extraordinarily large pearls. He pinned the corner of his poster and stepped back.

"Oscar Sheppard."

"This is my husband, Stephen." She gestured to a pudgy man in tweed. "We owe Dr. Sheppard money, Stephen. Dr. Sheppard, do you have a minute? Good. Let's feed you. You look hungry."

Mrs. Summer got the waiter with a look. She said, "Stoli, one rock, and my husband will have the chicken sandwich."

"And a side of mayo?" Stephen said.

"And a side of mayo—please bring it in a ramekin."

Dr. Sheppard ordered a white wine spritzer and the raw vegetable appetizer. Over their drinks, the Summers asked Dr. Sheppard questions about his flight, his wife, his books, and his appointment at Columbia. He told them about Isabel and their shared practice. He explained that she didn't like the big meetings or travel, and he praised Debbie's intelligence.

"I think our sessions are going very well."

"Oh, she says you're marvelous. Of course, she doesn't show any improvement, as far as I can tell, but these things take time, one supposes."

"Yes, she's just barely started on the medication."

"Barely started." Kitty snorted.

"Generally speaking, it takes a month for the brain to—"

"Ah."

The waiter put Stephen's sandwich and mayonnaise in

front of him. Mrs. Summer took two Ziploc bags out of her purse. She put the bread in one, and the lettuce and tomato in the other. She put both bags back into her purse, picked up a knife, dipped the tip of it into the mayonnaise, dotted the chicken, and put the knife back down precisely.

"How long are you in town?" she asked.

"Till Sunday."

"Oh, that's too bad. We could have had you over for dinner, but at least you'll have time to go to the baths. Have you been yet? I don't really go in for museums. Do you? What do you go in for?"

Dr. Sheppard told Mrs. Summer about some of his hobbies. He worked out three times a week, he explained, and he was devoted to daily meditation. Kitty loved horses. While they talked about her prize-winning dressage, her husband ate. When he choked on a bit of his chicken, Mrs. Summer gave him a glass of water. "It's the mayonnaise," she explained to Dr. Sheppard.

"At home, I have my riding. But this year, during Stephen's appointment, I've decided I'm taking time off. So today, for example, I did a little shopping."

"Appointment?"

"Stephen is a diplomat," Mrs. Summer said.

"Ambassador Summer?"

"Head ass-kisser Summer," Stephen said. "My wife fund-raised for the last campaign, and this is the reward."

"Well, it must be nice."

"Hmph. I spend half my day managing the Dunleavys."

"Stephen is talking about our caretakers in St. Louis.

They're a charming couple, but they've never really been in service. I called last week asking them to take a bag of mine out of storage and mail it to Debbie, and they behaved as if it was a great inconvenience."

"They haven't met Kitty yet," Stephen said to Dr. Sheppard, and raised his eyebrows. It seemed like he was issuing a friendly warning.

Dr. Sheppard changed the subject. "Does your daughter mind you being away for a year?"

"Are you putting us on the couch, Dr. Sheppard?" Mrs. Summer laughed. Stephen smiled politely. Mrs. Summer said, "I think she's glad. She has the opinion that I control her life."

"She never mentioned that."

"She wouldn't. She's too cunning." She stopped herself and then said, "When Debbie moved to New York, I came up and helped her get settled. We looked at apartments together, and when we found one she liked—emphasis on *she liked*, that girl, well, we're the ones who made her that way—we bought furniture. I didn't think about it when she didn't thank me because children tend to expect you to do that kind of thing, but three years later she called me blind drunk and told me that I was crazy and I'd ruined her life because I bought her three sets of kitchenware. Of course, the parents are always to blame. I'm boring you?"

"No."

"You think it's odd that Stephen is eating boiled chicken. I'm sorry, it's his diet."

"No, I understand. But can I ask, why do you have the bags?"

"My baggies? You pay for the lettuce and tomato and bread whether you eat it or not, so I take it and put it in the fridge for Tove. Dr. Sheppard? While we're on the subject of diet and exercise, I think it's important that Debbie doesn't know we've met. Stephen, you agree. She would regard it as a betrayal. I bought her kitchen supplies and she still hasn't forgiven me."

Back in the office, Debbie brought him a small cake from Dean & DeLuca. He worried about normalizing this kind of behavior. He watched as she sliced the cake in half, and he let her serve him a slice, but he took only a very small bite and then put it down.

"How was your weekend?" Debbie asked.

"It was all right."

"You look like shit, no offense. What did you do?"

Dr. Sheppard looked at his telephone. He righted his prescription pad so that it was in line with his blotter and said, "I went to New Haven."

"Oh, why?"

"I had my thirty-year reunion."

"Did you drink too much?"

"Very funny."

Debbie took small bites of her cake. She ate daintily, but without any shame. His gaze drifted toward her thighs, which were spread out flat on the armchair, and looked like elephant trunks.

"I'm just asking because I've never seen you look so tired," she said. "I mean, that's the polite word for it. You look like somebody beat you."

"I flew home on a redeye."

"Redeye from New Haven?"

Dr. Sheppard blushed. Debbie took a bite of cake and put her plate down. She'd eaten almost half a slice.

"Well. Did you have fun?"

"I saw old friends."

"See anyone I'd know? I know lots of people in New Haven. Not that I'm like a New Haven asshole. I went to Bowdoin. I got into Yale, but fuck them. I hate those people. I honestly do."

She looked at her cake slice.

"Do you know the name David Kehn? He's an old roommate of mine."

"Senator David Kehn? That guy's so gay."

"We lived together freshman and sophomore years, until he joined the art frat."

"But you're like prehistorically aged, no offense. I mean, you're very attractive. But he looks like twenty years younger than you. Did you two get high?"

"Yes, occasionally we did."

"Ha! My dad is going to freak out."

"Why don't you tell me what you did over your weekend?"

"Oh Christ."

Dr. Sheppard waited. Debbie said, "If you want to know, I hung out with friends."

"Tell me about your friends."

"Just friends. I hung out with Emily and Trip and Amol. Emily came over and—she does this thing, whenever she comes into my house, the first thing she does is, she says, 'I have to go to the bathroom.' It's so weird. It's like, what the fuck?

Once she went in there and a couple minutes later the fire alarm starts going off."

"I don't understand."

"She'd lit a match to cover up the smell of her shit, and she was so uptight about it she put the match in the bin full of Kleenex and started a fire. I mean, and I'm the one on medication."

Debbie laughed, and Dr. Sheppard watched her.

"I'm not avoiding the question, if that's what you're suggesting with that expression. Emily came over and we opened a bottle of wine. Trip called and invited us to the Wonkey Donkey—that's this loft—so we went over there, and they had some red wine and vodka, so we made Stalins. Have you been drinking Stalins, come to think of it? You look like it, no offense. That was a joke. You can laugh any time. It's not a job interview. So anyway, Emily passed out up in Trip's loft, and Gandalf drank red wine out of my shoe, then I fooled around with Amol, and around sunrise Emily woke up and I got us a cab back home and she stayed over in my bed. Amol's dad was a spy, or so he says. He's a pianist. Sunday afternoon me and Emily watched HBO, and around ten I figured she wasn't leaving, so I ordered us Indian food and opened a bottle of wine, and then we went around the corner to Scratchers. My relationship to Amol is a secret, by the way. Not even Emily knows. So we went to Scratchers and I asked this guy if I could look in his wallet, and it was full of old ticket stubs, so I told him he had a broken heart."

"What?"

"Seeing movies alone means you have a broken heart."

"How'd you know he saw them alone?"

"I asked him. Okay, your turn. Is Senator Kehn gay? I have a bet with my brother he's gay."

Dr. Sheppard looked at the ceiling and pressed his palms to his eyes. "Do you think maybe you could ask me something else?"

"Yeah. Why not." She thought for a moment. "Okay. Here's a good one. Do you look at pornography online?"

"Sure. I think we all do, these days."

"And . . . ?"

"And what? I usually have trouble finding the kind of thing I like, because I don't want to sign up for any of the websites. It takes me a long time, looking at those tiny pictures."

"Little pictures?" She laughed. "What kind of connection do you have, a dial-up?"

Dr. Sheppard shrugged. "I have a good connection."

"Well, you know about free porn, right?"

"I look at DogFart. You can find those on Brazzers."

"Whoa."

He shrugged. "Does that make you uncomfortable?"

"It's just weird to hear someone say it out loud." She was quiet for a while. "It's like even the word 'Facebook' is embarrassing. But how do you have trouble finding what you like? It's got everything. You must be into something totally weird."

"What's weird?"

"Mm, I guess rape?"

"That's a pretty common fantasy, especially among my clientele." He smiled conspiratorially.

"Right, but it's hard to find on . . ." Debbie trailed off.

"What made you ask the question?"

"Oh, I don't know. It wouldn't be appropriate to talk about it with you."

Dr. Sheppard blinked.

"I can see that you can't tell when I'm joking. That's kinda funny, isn't it? Because you should be able to read me by now. That's like your job. Anyway, I just was thinking about porn because I used to never look at it, but since I broke up with Tom, I'm not having sex with anybody, and then you started me on these medications and my sex drive changed or something, and I started having less sex, like no sex drive at all, which weirded me out, so I started off with online porn, basically nothing, but in about a day I fell down a rabbit hole, and now I look at the totally fucked-up stuff, and I feel weird about it. I heard about this crazy vibrator and I got one, and now I'm spending hours each morning with it. Sorry. But still, I feel just kind of weird about it. I thought we're supposed to be honest. Did I gross you out?"

"Well, I wouldn't say it's normal."

"I feel like a sex addict or something."

Dr. Sheppard shrugged. He didn't point out the obvious, that she wasn't having sex. It wasn't out of a therapeutic agenda. It was because he felt uncomfortable. He was feeling turned on. That was unusual. He had many female clients, and most spent all their time in session discussing their sex lives and their romantic lives, and the ways those two things made them miserable. He had heard a lot of things. He did not usually shy away from the subject of sex.

Debbie got up and started packing his barely touched slice of cake in the box.

"Are you going to take that home and eat it?" Dr. Sheppard asked.

An angry expression flashed across Debbie's face. She said, "I was putting it in the box for you."

It was unseasonably hot, 90 degrees in April. Dr. Sheppard was regretting a text he had sent Isabel the night before. He had been drinking at the bar below his apartment, and he'd had the opportunity to sleep with an attractive young woman. She was twenty-three years old. He had texted Isabel to tell her. It was too embarrassing to look at the exact words. When his phone rang, he expected to be excoriated.

"Dr. Sheppard? Kitty here. Do you have a minute? Good. I'm calling because I'm concerned. I was in New York last weekend and I saw Debbie. We had given her a hammer—to be more precise, her younger brother had given it to her—and it was covered in rubber cement and paint, and I don't know what all else. Apparently she'd loaned it to one of her bohemian friends? And a chair from the set I bought her was missing. I asked her about it, of course, and she told me she'd broken it apart for kindling. Now, Dr. Sheppard, I don't want to get into a discussion about money, but what exactly is it we're paying for?"

"Well, Debbie doesn't seem to have a lot of friends."

"She's out with friends every night."

"Oh, I mean she has Trip and Emily and Amol—people she gets drunk with. Emily is all right, if a little hysterical. And Trip seems like he basically shares some of her background. But I don't really care for this Amol. From what I can gather, he's an editor or a pianist or something."

"Oh God. This is appalling."

"What? I've offended you."

"The fucking pianist-errant."

"The penis what?"

"Amol. He was accepted to Harvard Law, but he heard another student playing jazz music and he dropped out and moved to Morocco. Now he has a piano strapped to a pickup, and the last time I heard, it had rolled off and smashed up a Camaro."

"You mean the Wonkey Donkey." He laughed. "Well, that one's a bit complicated, actually."

"She's seeing him?"

"They 'hook up.' Let me recommend an essay to you. It's by Tom Wolfe, called 'Hooking Up.' It basically explains it to our generation."

"Why are they so crazy about romance, Dr. Sheppard? I mean, you and I, we understood, it's not about expression or freedom but finding someone who cultivates your dignity. Like Stephen for me, or Isabel for you. That's all marriage is. What is it with these kids wanting to be artists?"

It was with the intention of reassuring her that he had begun, but when she mentioned Isabel, it caught him off guard, and he told her, "She was a beautiful woman. She is a beautiful woman. We're separated, you know. Or I guess you don't know that. It's not something I talk about, outside therapy. And then all our friends are scared of me now."

"The lone wheel?"

"The what?"

"You don't have a place, a position in the world, so naturally they're nervous."

Two hours later they were still talking, and he had told Kitty everything that he knew about Debbie.

Over the next year, their shared secrets evolved into a bond. They conspired. Kitty called to ask about Debbie; he waited for those calls. Sometimes he texted if there was a problem that was pressing, and within a few minutes his phone rang.

Debbie improved. She went from a size ten to a size four. She was still too big to borrow clothes from her mother, but she began to dress like a woman. She wore dresses, and when she did wear an oxford shirt, it was bright white and starched, and she wore it with tight jeans and riding boots.

But Debbie didn't seem to be aware that her shoes were unpolished. It was a pity, because anyone could see at a glance that all of her boots were exceptionally fine—some designer and some handmade. He didn't know how to bring it up. During meditation one morning, he caught himself envisioning a trial. He was on the witness stand, defending himself. "And why," a female lawyer asked, "did you choose that expression?"

•

"What are you over there thinking about?" Debbie asked.

"Oh, I was thinking about an apartment. I made an offer on an apartment. The seller accepted it. I'm supposed to hear later today if I can buy."

"A loan."

"No, it isn't a loan." He stopped himself. He hadn't told Debbie that he and his wife were separated, and he didn't know how to now. It wasn't a secret he had meant to keep, but now he had known her for more than a year, and it seemed funny to say all at once that he was in the midst of a property settlement and divorce. He said, "What were you thinking about?"

"Oh, nothing."

He waited. She said, "When you make that face, I have to tell you what I'm thinking." And then she was quiet again. "Do you have bad credit or something?"

He let that go. He said, "Have you ever heard of shoe polish?"

"I don't go in for patent leather."

Dr. Sheppard looked at his shoes. "It's a parade gloss. But you really can't treat your shoes like that; it's bad for the leather. Look." He got down to show her. He lifted her shoe and turned it. "See this cracking you're getting? You literally slap these shoes against the ground into water, salt, dirt, grease, and grime thousands of times a day. It's not like your skin— the leather of your shoes only receives the nourishment you give it."

She let him handle her legs and boots.

"Did you even condition these after you bought them? Surely your mother did."

He went around to his desk and opened the top drawer. He dug around. "Shit," he said.

"Dr. Sheppard."

"Hold on—stay here, I'll be right back."

He went up front and came back a few minutes later with two rags and a jar of Vaseline. He closed the door.

"Don't start with me," he said, and he got down on his knees and worked Vaseline into her right and then her left boot. She was quiet while he worked.

When he was done, she said, "Thank you."

"Oh." He waved a hand dismissively, but he couldn't think of anything else to say.

Dr. Sheppard was talking to Kitty while lying on the couch of his office. He said, "Kitty, I took them off her feet before polishing them."

"Well, for chrissake, yes. I should hope so. I mean, I presumed. But nevertheless. Wait, *you* took them off? You mean she took them off."

"Yes, naturally. She did. Anyway, I brought up marriage with her."

"Did she attack you?"

"No, actually. She cried. She asked me how she could meet men."

"Good. What'd you tell her?"

"I told her, you know." Dr. Sheppard didn't want to lie

again, but the truth was, he wasn't sure what Kitty wanted to hear. "I told her that she had to be open to it."

"Open . . . She needs to get out of her apartment. She needs to lose a few."

"She's a size four!"

"I know, I know, with Trish, the Paltrow nutritionist. Do you believe Gwyneth had a fat ass? That's the kind of thing a savvy woman can conceal. But I told her you can't be on twelve hundred calories. It's just not effective. I want a daughter who can wear belts."

"I don't know, Kitty. There's a limit. Apparently Trish is over there measuring out servings of butter. I don't eat butter, myself. My trainer doesn't encourage it, but I mean, I think apart from the butter, she's doing all she can."

"Don't knock butter. Butter isn't a problem food. The problem foods are fruits and veggies. If you start in on one of those party platters, there's no stopping. Watch next time you're at one of your little . . . functions. The fatties gather around the celery. I don't touch it."

"What, may I ask, do you eat?"

"Whataburgers. I have one a day."

"Kitty Summer eats Whataburgers?"

"It works. I order them dry. If I'm very hungry, I'll get a packet of mayonnaise."

"Like with your husband in Stockholm."

"And then on my birthday I eat an entire white cake."

"Dr. Sheppard? It's me. Can you talk? It's late here."

He looked at his watch. It was after nine, so it would be

3 a.m. in France. He was still at the office, but for all Debbie knew, he was at home. For all she knew, his wife could have been right beside him.

"Who is this?" Dr. Sheppard said.

"It's Debbie. Like you don't know," Debbie said. "You're the worst. But hold on. I've gotta keep my voice down. My mother's drunk. Hold on."

He heard Debbie shuffling around. She said, "I'm back."

"How is France?"

"France is cool. I mean, it's okay. You know how it is, you get to the hotel and after about an hour there's nothing to do but drink. It's hard to actually enjoy it. Listen, is it okay that I'm calling you? I miss you."

"Is there an emergency . . ."

"It's weird, I think I need a session. Can you do a telephone session? What time is it there? Are you in the office still? It's late here. Are you already at home? Are you in bed or something?"

"What was it you wanted to discuss?"

"I thought about you when I was taking my shoes off at security."

Dr. Sheppard settled down into his chair.

"Are you there?"

"I'm here."

"This security guard. Well, I mean, I thought about you on the plane, too. Hold on."

Dr. Sheppard recognized the vacuum pull and clink of little bottles—she was in the minibar. He heard her unscrew and pour—was it three or four, surely three—bottles.

"I'm back. What were we saying? 'What wuz we sayin.'

Oh. Yeah, you're in trouble, man. I saw David Kehn and he doesn't even go to reunions, plus he said you already had your thirty-fifth."

"Debbie, are you mixing alcohol with your medication?"

"Hey, and speaking of which— No, Mom! I'm talking to Emily!" she yelled. Then she whispered into the phone: "She wants me to come back and watch *Steel Magnolias* with her. Hold on, I'll be right back—well, no, you can come with me."

Dr. Sheppard heard Debbie fumble with a door and curse. Then he heard a stream of water. It was interrupted by a toot. Debbie laughed, and finished peeing. She flushed the toilet.

"Debbie, are you all right?"

"Shh! I can talk in here in the bathroom. I locked the door and she can't hear."

"Why?"

"Don't worry; it's not weird. It's like the size of your whole office. It's got a swimming pool. It's got a Jacuzzi. The swimming pool here is carved out of the mountain. It's the best. You've got to come here sometime. We could come together if that wouldn't be weird."

Kitty was calling Dr. Sheppard on his other line. He said, "Debbie, could you hold on for a second."

"Sure, I'll just sit here on the bathroom floor. Maybe I'll start a bath. For when we get off, I mean. Is that your wife?"

"Just a second."

"It's another patient?"

He switched over.

"Oscar? I'm sorry to call so late, but I'm worried about Debbie. She's very drunk. Is she calling you?"

"Hi."

"Debbie's not on the other line, is she?"

"No."

"Of course. It sounded like you were on the other line, and my daughter's drunk and hiding in the toilet. Listen. I've got a little questionarooni. I don't know how to put it delicately."

Debbie must have hung up and called him again: he had a call.

"Kitty, I have another call. Do you think maybe I could call you back?"

"I'll hold."

Dr. Sheppard switched over.

"Did you hang up on me? I'm just getting in the bath; I don't care. It's not weird. Who was that? You're always so weird. It's not very fair. Which is my point. I mean, that's why I'm calling, about this marriage thing, because I need to know. I don't want you to give me your professional act. What's up? Why do you see me?"

"It is my job."

"Cut the shit."

"Debbie."

"You're a liar."

Kitty had hung up and redialed. Dr. Sheppard said, "Can you hold on, I have this patient on the other line. It will just be a second."

He was so anxious that he made a mistake. He thought he had switched over, but he hadn't. He still had Debbie on the line. He said, "I lied a moment ago. I'm going to level with you: I have Debbie on the other line."

"Still me," Debbie said. "What a total fucking giveaway. It is your wife! Listen, I'm running a bath, is that cool? If your wife's jealous I'm calling, just tell her I'm crazy. You should be home, anyway. It's late. Are you in the office? 'Tell me what you're wearing.' That's a joke! Do you do phone sex with your wife? Can you do a session with me if I'm naked?"

Kitty's call went to voicemail. She never left a message. He wondered if she would call again. A text message rolled in. It was from Kitty. It said, "I'm lying in bed right now and you're all I can think about."

She sent a second. "Tell me to take off my panties."

The other line beeped. It was Kitty. He said, "Can you hold on for one second?" and switched over.

"Dr. Sheppard, have you ever really been fucked?"

"Could you hold on a second?"

He switched back to Debbie and said, "Debbie, I think we should discuss this in my office. I appreciate that you've been honest, but I worry this isn't the time for us to have this sensitive of a, of a, of a . . . discussion."

"Look, Dr. Sheppard. Let's just tell the truth for once. I fucking love you, okay. I love you. I think about you all the time. I mean, tell me I'm wrong. I fucking talk about you. I fucking think about you. I jerk off to you. I'm sorry. Jesus, I'm sorry. I heard it's transference. It's transference, that's why I think about you—I'm messed up. I'm totally showing you my shit here. I'm fucked up. But the truth is, you're in love with me, too. I know it. And you're in love with my mother, which is fucking insane."

"It isn't transference," Dr. Sheppard said. "Our connection is real."

"Oh good. Oh, that's really good. I know it is."

"But I think it would be wise of us to discuss this at a different time."

"I know I know I know," Debbie said. "I know. Don't start all that. What I want to know is, did you tell my mother you polished my shoes."

"No."

"Because that was this privately totally cool thing between us, and you can't fucking share it with her. She's so fucked up. Now she's like jealous of me, because I'm not a size ten anymore and I can basically wear her fucking belts, and she's—old. Like I give a shit about her belts or the fucking maître d'. You know? But it's like a contest—who can nail the maître d'. 'Fucking take the fucking—' Jesus, is it my fault he comes on to me? I mean, who gives a fuck about the maître d', Dr. Sheppard."

"Debbie, can I have confidence you won't hurt yourself?"

"You think I'm suicidal?"

"I mean, could you stop drinking and taking pills for the night."

Debbie hung up the phone. He switched over, and Kitty said, "Hello."

•

Dr. Sheppard came down with the flu, and had to miss three appointments with Debbie. When he saw Debbie again, he was scared. He didn't know how to proceed. She looked good. She was wearing jeans and a polo shirt, and she had gotten sun. She even had some freckles on her breastbone.

She said, "I want to apologize for calling you, and for the things I said. I'd had a lot to drink, and I wasn't really myself."

"Oh, it wasn't anything serious." Dr. Sheppard waved a hand. "I mean, you don't need to apologize."

"I feel like I do. I mean, I was serious. Everything that I said was true."

"I don't think I follow."

"I'm in love with you."

"Sweetheart, you just don't have any real friends."

"I have a ton of friends."

He raised his eyebrows.

She said, "What difference does it make?"

He argued that her love came out of loneliness, and she argued that all love came out of mutual loneliness. She said, "The deeper the loneliness, the deeper the love."

She stood up. She picked up one of his Satsuma vases and threw it. Her aim was excellent, and it soared across the room toward the large window. It hit the window, bounced off, and landed on the carpet. Dr. Sheppard had expected it to shatter, but he stood and went around the desk and found it unharmed. He picked it up and held it.

Debbie was looking for something else to throw. She picked up a glass vase of cut lilies—a gift from one of his divorced patients—and chucked it against the wall. It sprayed dirty, rotten flower water across his desk, across the wall and the front of his shirt, but the vase did not break. It landed on the hardwood floor, the flowers still inside.

"Debbie," Dr. Sheppard said. "Debbie."

She turned over an end table and lunged for his other Satsuma vase. This one she raised above her head with both arms and threw down onto the hardwood floor. One of the handles broke off.

Abruptly, unexpectedly, she got a hold of herself. She looked around. She said, "I've got to go." Then her mouth turned down involuntarily twice. She opened the door to his office and said, "Let's go."

"Is something the matter?" a woman's voice said.

"He said we can't see each other anymore."

"Whatever for?"

Dr. Sheppard recognized Kitty's voice. She said, "Debbie, hon. Debbie? Where are you going?"

Kitty was in the waiting room of his office. It was 11 a.m. and spring, but she wore stiletto-heeled boots, skin-tight leather pants, a cropped band jacket, and a matching polka-dot necktie and blouse. His secretary eyed Kitty with fear and anticipation. She had watched Debbie storm out and was no doubt looking forward to a show.

"Dr. Sheppard," Kitty said, "Debbie charged off . . ." She smoothed her hair. "Why are you holding that vase?"

He realized he had the undamaged vase in his arms. He sat down with his arms wrapped around it. Kitty sat down next to him.

Kitty said, "I'm a little confused."

"So am I."

She smoothed her hair a second time. "Ever since we spoke in France, you haven't been answering my calls."

"I'm sorry, Kitty. It's been a very busy time. My school responsibilities have been onerous. I'm a bit overwhelmed."

"Is this because of what happened between the two of us?"

Dr. Sheppard cringed. "I'm not sure what you're referring to. I'd like to discuss Debbie with you, Kitty. But I'm afraid I can't, as it would violate patient-doctor confidentiality. You understand that."

"Patient-doctor what?"

"Confidentiality. My professional ethics."

Kitty nodded. "Of course."

She stood up to go. Then she paused. She turned.

She said, "There's something I've always meant to ask you, Dr. Sheppard. Since we're speaking as professionals."

"Ask anything." He shrugged, and put the vase on the coffee table.

"Why did your wife leave you?"

He started to explain to her about his professional success, and Isabel's suggestion that he was arrogant. Before he could fully express his thoughts, Kitty said, "Isabel is a very beautiful woman. I think it's much simpler than all that, Dr. Sheppard. Did you ever think it might have had something to do with your being fat?"

"I'm—I beg your pardon?"

The conversation wasn't going well. It would be better to go back to his office. Kitty caught him as he rounded the coffee table. He kept his arms around the vase. She pushed him down onto the couch.

He tried to get back up, and Kitty grabbed his shoulders. He shoved her, and the vase fell to the ground, but it did not break. She punched him in the throat. He fell backward onto the couch. Kitty must have taken self-defense classes. He was having trouble breathing. She gathered her handbag from his desk, brushed her hair with one hand.

She turned on a heel and strode out. As she was opening the door, he said, "You cunts."

She turned her head slightly, but caught herself. He read the expression on her face. She was fascinated.

Night Report

After they made love he said, "Ema, I've been reading a new book. Well, it's an old book, but no one knows about it anymore. It's a great book, though writing it ruined the author's career. She's a fascinating woman—she was—Sloane Newam, do you know her?"

"I've heard the name," Ema said. "I think I read something by her—she wrote that thing about a television show, didn't she?"

"*Night Report on ABC*. But the book is about a whole network!"

"That's right. *Night Report*, that thing, bum-BUM-bum."

"You would like this Sloane Newam. She's funny. She reminds me of you."

"What do you mean?"

At the airport the next day, he gave her a copy of Sloane Newam's memoir and said, "Read it and you will see."

She began reading in the line at check-in. Halfway through the novel, flying over Missouri, she came to a fight between Sloane Newam and the head of her network. Mid-sentence, Sloane Newam wrote, "This may be the wrong time to say that I loved him. I did." Ema pressed the book to her chest.

"Are you all right?" the woman beside her asked.

Ema wiped her cheeks and nodded. She turned away from the woman. She'd drunk several small bottles of scotch. She didn't want to be rude, so she turned back to face the woman and said, "It's pretty, huh? Out the window. It's Missouri. Get it? Mis-uh-ry? Misery. It's like—I'm so happy, I'm over misery—Missouri. Ha."

The woman seemed embarrassed and turned away.

Sloane Newam had written two novels. They were out of print. One was on sale on Amazon for a penny, plus shipping, and the other was priced at $109. Ema ordered both.

They came the day before Christmas. Ema made her champagne sorbet. It was made by pouring two bottles of champagne into a bowl and putting it into the freezer, then stirring every half hour. She ate her champagne sorbet from the bowl, in bed with a spoon, and read Sloane Newam's novels.

The second was about Sloane Newam's lifelong affair with a married man. Sloane Newam had captured what Ema could not. She had captured the way loving someone who wasn't there made the world seem funny and enchanted.

Was the married man trying to tell her this? Ema didn't

think so. She didn't think the married man had read the novels, and if he had, it was unlikely he would understand them. For him the affair was an escape valve. For her it was poetic. She had once tried to tell him, "You are in the fabric of everything I see. When I see three young men in denim jackets, I am already describing it to you. Before I describe it to myself, I am in a dialogue with you." He hadn't been able to make it out to L.A. for a few months after that.

But Sloane Newam expressed it, because she barely talked about her married man at all. Instead, she described scenes from her life. She described being stranded at an airport in France, in the ticketing area outside of the terminal, and having to spend the night sleeping on a long bench with a group of French hobos. One offered her apple wine, and told the others, "She is normal. She is normal. Nothing happens to her." She told a story of a bat that flew into her bedroom and perched on the exposed-brick wall, and how she took him out by hand. Her novel was a defense of adultery, and a rejection of the commonsense stuff everyone spouted—that he had to get a divorce, that she had to leave him. Sloane Newam did neither. At the end of her novel she asked the married man, "Do you ever wish I was the one with you?" He said, "You are."

Ema completed that novel at 3 a.m., and she wrote a long text message to the married man. When she clicked send, her phone's screen went blank. She flipped from the main screen back to the message screen. It had lost her text!

Then the first two sentences of her text rolled up. They had gone through, she guessed, but the rest of the text was gone. Horrified, she reread the two lines. They were weird and alone-looking.

> I have been up reading *Fiber Optics, Holy Places*. I just finished it. It has this beautiful passage where she describes a kitten—she is Joan

Ema was confused. Two more lines from her text rolled up.

> Newam—on the streets of Varanasi. It is so incredibly amazing—she's there on assignment, and she's just been to prayers at the

Ema understood. The married man's old phone was cutting her single long text into twenty-one parts, of 144 characters each. She was powerless to stop it. She watched in a panic as another text rolled through, another 144 characters from her long text, to the married man in France.

In a panic, she turned off her phone to make it stop. She went to the oven, opened it, and leaned against the door. She could see into the bathroom and contemplated dropping her phone into the toilet. She turned it on, and waited.

She watched the screen as it loaded. She said, "Please. Please. Please."

Then the texts really started to roll.

> Ganges River, which she finds completely boring, and she's just been coughing in the incense smoke and body odor, and then she

sees this adorable homeless kitten, like a stick with some fur, and she's with the married man, and they look at each other and

know they have to take it—even though that's completely crazy. And the kitten is so skinny and it's actually in a puddy? so

they don't even realize till they get it back to the very expensive room which they splurged—and they're in this five-star

hotel, and have to bribe the man at the door, because they don't think to hide this mud-covered CAT—that the kitten's arm

is broken in three places. So they take it to the veterinary college the next day, and each of these darling, sweet Indian medical

students comes to feel the kitten's broken arm, you know they're studetnts right, and you can tell when they've found the break because

the kitten goes, "Mewl mewl mewl melw mewl mewl mwl mewl" and cries! So after about the fifth medical student squeezes the poor

thing's arm, Sloane steps in and tells them to stop it, absolutely enough, and of course it stops. And there are all these diagrams of cows right there on the wall, and a surgical theater, harness for the cows. But the diagrams are like colored in by a kid, and most rudimentary

things, but she realizes these students actually use them to navigate inside a cow. That these young men in coats go inside and surgeons

and so they have to shave her cat to the skin to amputate its arm because it's an old broken. And to shave it they ask her to hold the kitten

down, and he's terrified. She has him by his back, and the scruff of this is the worst thing that has happen, and when they've shave

the animal of his fur they ask if he has eaten any food at all in the past twenty-four hours, and Sloane and the man she is in love

with do not know, of course, so the cat can't have his surgery, and they take him home to the hotel, but he won't let them hold him

any longer. And then his arm removed, and he can make it through that, and she sneaks him home in this case, and he can make it

through that, but when**a month lateR**she has to go on
assignment to Haiti, it is the last thing the poor little animal

can take, she can't just leave him ALONE< and he goes off
into the woods to die. Like Jesus into the dessert, she
writes, and I was just crying,

crying, crying, and all this time there's the mouse in my
house, chewing the stove, the one I told you about, so it's
like sometimes life can be so

beautiful.

In the morning, Ema woke up on the sofa. She had her shoes
on. She woke up innocent, then remembered the night before.
She lunged for her phone.

At 5:15 a.m. the married man had answered all of her texts
with two words, "Good times." And then, several hours later,
he had texted: "While I'm out of the country, email is best.
I'm sorry. Roaming rates are insane. x"

Ema put a listing on Craigslist, to sublet her apartment,
and she registered for a monthlong meditation program in the
mountains of Vermont. The program began in three days, and
her apartment was sublet by noon. This struck her as a sign.

Just after dawn, Ema rolled up her sleeping bag. She stored
her foam mattress in the attic above the shrine room. Still in

her pajamas, she went down past the lower living room, where several people sat in armchairs drinking tea, and an old woman with the body of a classically trained dancer did her morning stretches. Ema paused for a moment and watched her. The woman looked familiar. Out in the rock garden, a bearded man ran a rake in a circle through the pebbles around a large rock. Ema went to the service area off the dining hall and poured herself coffee.

At six they met in the main shrine room. There were forty of them. They sat overlooking a valley. At the bottom of a nearby hillside was a manmade turtle and lotus pond. The pads were flowerless in the muddy water, which was golden in the morning light. The *umdze* rang the gong and they stood and walked in circles around the shrine room, their right hands in the palms of their left.

Bill was the *dhathun* leader. He had a long face and gray hair, and he was tall. He had put on a shirt and tie. They were in the dining room, and it was just after 2 p.m., and he sat on the meditation cushion on the floor. "Is this anybody's tea?" he asked. "Can everyone see me okay?"

"I can't see," Ema said. She stood up. "I can see now."

"Okay." Bill clacked two pieces of wood together. "So, when you hear that sound, that means you bow, and you untie your set."

He bowed.

"You might want to follow along," he said, and he looked at Ema.

Ema sat down. She said, "Are we supposed to come up after the bow? Or do we just go straight down."

"Just go straight down." Bill made the gesture again. He bowed, bent down farther, and untied his oryoki set. He said, "What's nice about this knot is, if you do it right, it just pulls apart. It's a slipknot."

"How do you tie that?"

"You start out like this." He laid his left hand, palm up, on top of his set.

"Wait. Can you do that again, this time so I can see it?"

"Well, you might want to stand up."

"I can't stand up and do the knot," Ema said. "That's what I said at the beginning, but you wouldn't listen."

"Okay, okay."

He untied and retied the knot for her twice, then moved on to the second knot, and then he stopped short.

"I made a mistake. I'm sorry. Okay, now, actually, I forgot. The first thing we'll do is, you'll hear the ding, and then you'll go and get tables. Now, there're a lot of variations on that, and you'll hear a million different ways, so let's just say that the fourth member of the quadrant gets up, goes to the head of the quadrant, bows, and walks down the line to the back of the shrine room."

"Do you bow first?" Ema asked.

"What do you mean first?"

"Before you go and get the tables."

"You bow first," Bill said.

"I know that, but where do you bow? At the front or at the back?"

"At the head. Now," he said, lifting the wipe serviette, "you want to take this ratty dirty thing here and fold it in half, then fold it in a trifold."

"I can't see," Ema said.

Bill extended both arms high above his head, and he repeated himself, demonstrating the fold.

"But normally, of course, you're going to want to do this with your hands held a little lower."

"A comedian," Ema said.

"What?" The dancing-stretching woman gave Ema a look that struck to her core. She said, "Some of us want to learn."

"I was just kidding."

"Some of us have dexterity issues," an elderly woman said.

"Some of us have just plain issues," the dancing-stretching woman murmured, and everyone laughed, except Bill and Ema.

Bill said, "So once you've got your wipe serviette folded, you're gonna want to take that in your left hand and set it down before you. Then you're gonna want to pick up your *setsu* case with your left hand and rotate that forty-five degrees, and set that down under your wipe serviette." He shook his bowl out as he went on. "We always want to pick up bowls with our two thumbs," he began. "Tell me if you can do that."

"Uh, no. No, I can't do that," the dancer woman said. "Carpal tunnel. Lifetime of typing!" She turned to all the retreatants and said, "Use ergonomic keyboards!"

"I can't do it either," the elderly woman said. "Could you explain it better? I don't think we're getting it."

•

After two weeks, during a break, Bill came and sat beside Ema. The dancer-stretcher was on the floor with her heel to her cheek. After some small talk, Ema said, "How long does it take to do a thousand prostrations?"

"Not very long," the dancer-stretcher said, even though no one asked her. She said, "About two, or two and a half hours."

"It always took me longer," Bill said. "Boy, you're flexible."

"Well, either way," Ema said, "that's a long time to stay focused."

"But it really isn't," the dancer-stretcher said. "I mean, when you think about it." She flopped forward to full splits and tapped her forehead to the carpet. Ema thought she had to be at least fifty-five.

"Who said I was focused?" Bill said.

"I did ngondro two times," the dancer-stretcher said. "I did the Drukpa Kagyu *ngondro* and the Longchen Nying-thig."

"So you've done, in your life, two hundred thousand prostrations?" Bill asked.

The dancer gave a short nod. "The first time, I did them too fast—I was told to. The second time, I did them slower, and that was better. The first time, it was too much. We had armed gunmen come into the place where we were practicing."

"Oh my God."

"It was *too* much."

"What did they do?"

"They tied us up and kicked us around." She held her hands as though she had a machine gun. "It was too much. But then we called up this lama, and he did a *mo*, and he said it was okay to go on."

A blind woman came and sat on Ema's other side. She dipped her tea bag methodically in a cup of hot water and turned her eyes from person to person.

"Hey," Ema said to the dancer, "I've been meaning to ask you this, because I saw you sleeping in the shrine room at first, and then I didn't. Where're you sleeping?"

"I'm sensitive to the heating system," the dancer said. "I have a secret place."

"Where?"

The blind woman laughed.

"What?" the dancer said.

The blind woman said, "Nothing. Just, you know. 'The secret place.' I think we all have one."

The dancer lifted one shoulder. She said, "Gross."

Ema would have grilled the dancer, but apropos of nothing, the blind woman began to ask Bill about the nature of reality. The blind woman wore color-coordinated outfits, and Ema always wanted to ask her how she did it. The blind woman offered reiki during breaks, and Ema kept meaning to sign up so she could get her alone and ask the secret. Probably just something on her tags.

"If it's all a dream . . ." The blind woman was talking to Bill. She had her face pointed at him. She said, "If I'm not real, then what about science? What about objective truth and reproducible scientific data?"

"But that could be a dream, as well," the dancer said.

The blind woman turned to face the dancer-stretcher and said, "Sloane, think about it. Someone does an experiment in one place, and a hundred years later, in an entirely different place, it can be done again with the same results. How is that a dream? Fusion has been taking place on the sun before humans existed, so how is the atom bomb imagined."

"Your name is Sloane?" Ema asked. She had a funny feeling.

"But all of that is in your mind," the dancer said. "Sloane Newam. You're Ema, right? Nice to meet you." She rolled through the splits, then bent her knees and arched her back to touch the balls of her feet to her forehead.

"That's impossible," Ema said.

"I think they're just two understandings of reality," Sloane Newam said. "Both are completely logical. See, in the Western sense, a subject precedes an object. Or I mean—sorry—an object precedes a subject."

"No, I mean it's impossible that you're Sloane Newam. I mean, *the* Sloane Newam? Sloane Newam the writer?" Ema said.

"Used to be, yes. Now I do yoga."

Sloane Newam rolled onto her neck and tried to touch her toes to the ground in front of her as she explained to the blind woman that, relatively, there were truths, but ultimately, there was nothing.

"I'm freaking out," Ema said. "The same Sloane Newam who interviewed Gorbachev?"

Addressing both Ema and the blind woman, Sloane

Newam got her feet onto the ground. She lifted herself to standing and said, "Take it like this. This table. When I reach out and touch it, I can't experience anything but my mind. I'm not experiencing a table, but rather, sense data—so-called touch, sight—is being transferred from my fingers to my brain."

"I'm seriously actually freaking out," Ema said. "Can everyone please be quiet?" She wanted to touch Sloane Newam.

But the blind woman seemed moved by what Sloane Newam had said. She touched the table and said, "So the scientific data is in my mind as well."

Ema let out a groan and stormed off.

It was a special day. In the shrine room, Bill had set up a large flat-screen TV, and on it was a ceremony for the teacher, who was going into a yearlong retreat. Sloane and Ema were servers, and sat outside the shrine room with group of five others serving the meal. Inside the shrine room, people watched the TV, for the most part, from cushions. They were seated Indian-style on the floor, and the mood was quiet and still, as though they were waiting to, or wondering if they would, feel something. The ceremony itself was being held in a gymnasium on the other side of the country. Twelve Asian women in brightly colored dresses were dancing. Ema still hadn't approached Sloane Newam to tell her the truth about what was happening. Whatever that truth might be—she herself wasn't sure.

"He is utterly liberated from the *skandhas*," the people

inside the shrine room began chanting. "He has cut the knots." Ema noticed that Sloane Newam was chanting, so she started to chant, too.

A server whom Ema had not noticed before stood abruptly and said, "Do we set the rice bowl down on the ground?"

"We hold it," Sloane Newam said.

"Exactly," Ema said.

"You hold their bowl?" The man was in his sixties, and he looked desperately panicked.

"No, the pot of rice."

"Right, of course."

"Rice," Bill said. It was the first time Ema had seen him flustered. "No! No. Not rice. No rice." He held a flat palm toward Sloane Newam, indicating she was not to stand.

"If you can't hold it," Sloane said, "kneel on one leg, and balance the pot on your knee."

Sloane Newam said, "Enter the shrine room with elegance."

There was a soft clacking sound. It was the blind woman.

"To the shrine," Bill said. "To the shrine, to the shrine."

"With elegance!"

"Do we bow?" the desperate man asked, and Sloane Newam pushed him forward. Ema was at the threshold to the shrine room when she realized all the people inside, hundreds of them, were singing, "Ema, the phenomena of the three worlds of samsara, not existing, they appear, how incredibly amazing." She stopped dead. She set the pot of rice on the ground. Then they all stared at her. They kept saying it! Were they crazy people? Did they think this was a *game*. "Who arranged this?" she said.

She saw Bill raise his eyebrows at Sloane Newam. Others of them looked confused, but they all kept staring at her and singing that song. She picked up the pot and went to a quadrant. It was a back one. You were supposed to start at the head. Some divorced guy was really enjoying this psycho gag. He was a bald loser, and now he was *smiling* at her, singing, "Ema, the phenomena, of the . . ."

"Cute," she said, and spooned rice into his bowl.

He lifted two fingers to indicate he'd had enough, and furrowed his brow. She spooned three more shovels of rice in his bowl. "Cute," she said. "Cute, yes, I see your fucking fingers. How incredibly amazing."

She went to the next woman, and she was at the third when Bill placed a hand on her shoulder.

"What happened?" he asked outside.

When she told him, he explained that they had been singing one of Milarepa's songs. Ema, in Tibetan, meant "How wonderful."

"I'm sorry," she said. "I have trust issues. I get these panic attacks, so if I seem weird, that's why. This is kind of like a nightmare to me, and I think maybe I should just—"

Sloane Newam walked up and put a hand on her shoulder. "Babe, it's why we chant. We chant each morning, 'May my confusion dawn as wisdom.' That's why."

Ema sat on a bench. As she began to put her shoes on, the tears started. She got up and walked back to Bill and Sloane.

"I'm having an anxiety attack," she said. "I'm having a breakdown." Her face twitched as she spoke, folding in at her cheeks, and the color rose up past her forehead, shading into her hairline. She knew when that happened that she looked like a samurai at the height of emotion in a kabuki play, and—in speaking the words—she had begun to cry harder. Sloane said, "Okay—okay," in a soft voice.

Bill said, "You go."

"It's only going to get worse," Ema said. "I know myself. I can't do it, so you guys better figure something out. I can't be here. I need to go away."

She went down to the women's changing room, where she sat in a plastic chair and, for a little over ten minutes, cried.

It was close to five, and almost dark outside. She got her cell phone from the pocket of her coat and turned it on. The house was quiet. It was empty. Everyone was in the shrine room, watching the time-delayed simulcast of the ceremony in Asia. In the dining room the tables were pushed against the wall. Lights floated in goblets of colored water, and globe-shaped paper lanterns were strung from the ceiling.

In the main office, two recent arrivals were looking around. One was in her late sixties. She was tall, healthy, and trim. She was tidy and debonair. The other was a man in his late thirties. He was handsome, with even features, large sympathetic eyes, and a beard that was just going gray. The office was spread with their baggage. They looked lost.

"Have you been checked in?" Ema asked.

"No." The woman was angry. "We've been standing here alone."

"I'll go and get someone," Ema said. "I wish I could help you, but I'm just a program participant, and I'm having a personal problem. I'm sorry, if you'll wait here—they're all—watching this thing. One minute."

"No," the woman said. She held up a piece of paper. "We're checked in."

"Oh." Ema was confused. "What are your names?"

"I am Alida and this is Francisco."

"Then I'm going to go and make a phone call."

In the parking lot it was possible sometimes to get cell phone reception. It took several attempts before she reached him. She cried, and she tried to tell him what had happened. She said, "They have some big ceremony. They're all in the shrine room. I didn't mean to be rude, but I just—"

"Ema, what are you doing?"

"What do you mean?"

"What are you doing? You hate New Age and you hate nature and you hate amateurs. But you've set yourself up with all three for a month, and you wonder why you're feeling bad."

"Oh God," she said. "It's good to hear an ordinary person. Sloane Newam is here. She's turned into some kind of contortionist know-it-all. She's the worst! And then there's a blind lady who does reiki."

"I've been reading her, too. You're right, she's a bit convoluted. But I'm glad you brought some good books to that place."

"No, for chrissake, she's HERE!" She started crying again. It was dark, and the parking lot's packed-sand surface was almost like asphalt. Ema tried to tell the married man about the real Sloane Newam, but the cell phone cut out. It went dead, and then it began playing a three-note error tone.

Sloane seemed to manifest from the darkness. She came

to a stop several inches closer than a friend would, and she said hello.

"Could you hear what I was saying?" Ema asked.

"I heard, 'Dee-dee-deep. Dee-dee-deep.' " She imitated the phone's error tone several more times.

"I was talking to the married man. It was a conversation I wouldn't want anyone else to hear."

"That's what married men are for," Sloane Newam said.

"What ever happened with yours?" Ema asked. "I mean, I read your novel."

Sloane Newam said, "I never wanted to do the obvious thing. It seemed to me like we had two choices. I would either ask him to get a divorce or I would leave him. I didn't see another option, but I didn't want to do the thing everyone does, so I didn't do either, and then he died."

Ema crumpled in a ball and clutched her knees. She said, "I hate this. I hate everything. I can't handle any more."

Sloane Newam touched her head. She said, "Think of the benefits of renunciation. Or if you prefer, contemplate the illusory nature of samsara, and appreciate that you have nothing to renounce."

"What?"

"Be skillful and practice whichever works for you at this very moment."

"At this very moment," Ema said, "I wish that I were dead. I'm heartbroken, and if I had a gun I would use it."

"Suicide is no escape. You must follow your karma."

"I would shoot you," Ema said. "And then I would go in there to that shrine room, and I would shoot Bill."

When she said that, it was so outrageous, she couldn't help feeling a little better. She said, "Then I'd shoot the blind lady."

"Eve."

"Yes, I'd shoot Eve. Thank you. I'd shoot Eve in the chest."

The Commission

He did not look like our ordinary client at Seibu. He was about fifty years old, and although his shirt was nicely pressed, his pants sat low under his stomach, with deep creases in a triangle around his lap area. It was early in the afternoon and the floor was almost empty, but the members of my sales staff were avoiding the client, pretending not to see him. This goes against our policy. For this reason, although it is not within my job description, I approached the client and offered him assistance. I prefer to lead by example.

"Can I help you find anything?" I asked.

"No," he said. "I'm finding everything okay."

He had a Southern gentleman's accent, and I could tell from the way he spoke that he was gay. Also, I couldn't help noticing that his teeth had plaque in the spaces between them, so that it looked like they were fusing into one tooth.

"I'll be just over here," I said. "Let me know if you need some assistance."

I had begun to walk away when he addressed me—"What price is this?"—and I turned to find him holding a Kuriki Tatsusuke tea bowl from the Gray collection.

"I don't know offhand," I said. "Would you like me to go and have a look?"

He indicated that he would, and so I said, "I'll just be one moment to check that price for you." All of our prices are kept on an inventory file. I had begun to cross the floor to access that file from Mr. Ito's station when the client said, "What's the point of it?"

"Sir?"

"The bowl." He flipped it to examine its bottom. "What do you use it for?"

"Oh, actually, it's a cup. For water or tea."

"Can you drink sake out of it?"

"Usually our sake cups are smaller, but of course, you are free to use that item for anything you like."

I think maybe I smiled a little, a habit of mine when I become uneasy. I had been reminded by my phrasing of the off-color stories that I've heard about gays. For a moment, I worried that the client thought I was making an offensive joke, but of course, he was not aware of any of this thinking on my part.

"Is it real gold?" He indicated the inside of the bowl.

"It's a glaze made with real gold, yes. Mr. Tatsusuke had a postdoctorate degree in chemistry, and he makes all his glaze himself."

"It is safe to drink from it?"

"Mr. Tatsusuke is very particular his work is to be used,

so I don't think he made anything with real gold inside that would come off when you try to drink it."

This is something that happens to me when I become nervous; my English begins to regress. While I have lived in America for forty years, I still have some of the irredeemable habits of a non-native speaker, particularly when I am shaken. I don't know why I had become shaken. I had noticed by this time the client was producing a particular odor, but I can't point to that and say, "This is how I was undone." It was a collection of things, and I suppose that I have fragile nerves. I said, "I'll go and check that price."

I went to Mr. Ito's computer. While I waited for the particular program to load, I glanced at the client. Alone with the bowl, he held it properly between his palms, and I had the impression that whatever he was imagining, it had led him to the decision that he would purchase the bowl, which was listed at $600.

It was a high price for a bowl, but Mr. Tatsusuke was enjoying a lot of success in Japan at that moment; he was in vogue. Actually, it was quite difficult to find his work, and we were able to stock it only because Mr. Tatsusuke had been a close personal friend of our company president, Mr. Seibu. In fact, he had even come to visit him in our store. A lovely man in his seventies, he arrived just wearing ordinary dungarees, and when he saw his pieces locked inside our jewelry cases, he got a little bit upset. He spent a lot of time with me personally, talking about the importance of touch. He said that a piece is beautified by being handled by all different sorts of hands, and he asked that I please place his work out, so people could touch it. He said, "I don't make art. I make bowls and plates."

I informed the client of the price, and he did not make any answer. He stood for a while admiring the bowl, picking it up and putting it down, and then he said he was going to think about it, and for a long time he wandered the store with his feelings painted all over his face. The other salespeople had grown accustomed to his appearance, and so for the most part, they were able to answer when he said, "What price is this?" regarding various store items, though I did hear Harry in menswear laughing.

What price is this, indeed.

It was half an hour later when I saw the client admiring the bowl again.

"Still thinking about that piece?" I asked.

He said something in a very soft voice. I couldn't make it out, so I nodded. He continued in the same train of thought, and I realized a few moments later that he had said, "I want it for a gift for my guru."

"This would make a very special gift," I said.

He nodded. Then he looked down into the bowl for a long time, and I was quiet, in accordance with my sales training. When he spoke again, the client expressed his wish to purchase the Tatsusuke.

"Good choice," I said. "Please come this way, sir."

I was careful to wrap the bowl very nicely for the client, Mr. Thibideaux, and before he left, I gave him my personal card. I think . . . sometimes I imagine that my husband watches me in my ordinary day. My son said this is ordinary to do. My son is a professional, Western-style therapist, and he said it is ordinary as long as I understand that my husband has passed away. I understand this; he is gone, and he will never come back—so sometimes in moments like this, I think my husband smiles, to see how kind and elegant his wife can be. Sometimes it is my husband, but he looks like Mr. Tatsusuke.

A month later, Mr. Thibideaux requested my assistance on the floor. I was in a meeting with our payroll chief, Mr. Hanson, but informed that a client had requested me by name, Mr. Hanson encouraged me to go ahead and assist the client. I found Mr. Thibideaux bent over a jewelry display with his stomach pressed against the glass.

"Mr. Thibideaux," I said, "how nice to see you again in our store."

He looked up at me from where he was and pointed out a headdress inside the case. "What price is this?"

I unlocked the case and withdrew the ornament. After I read its price, which was unusually high, I put the elaborate headpiece into Mr. Thibideaux's hands. He made a gesture, lifting the item up and down to indicate its weight. Then he asked if I would help him by trying it on.

"Excuse me? I'm sorry, I didn't understand."

He explained that he wanted me to try the headdress on. Actually, I had my hair pulled into a chignon, and I had no wish to perform this service. At the same time, I didn't wish to refuse Mr. Thibideaux impolitely. While I searched for words, Mr. Thibideaux began to ask me about the piece. It reminded him, he said, of Utagawa Hiroshige III's *Amerika*.

I was undone, and so I nodded and smiled in an uncomfortable way, my eyes most likely beginning to look confused, and blank.

He went on to explain it was a portrait of a foreign woman from the year 1860, done during a time when only twenty Western women lived in Yokohama. He explained that women in the West didn't wear plumed hats, but in portraits of Westerners painted in Japan, they were quite common. He asked if I would place the headdress on his head, explaining that it was really preferable to my wearing it, because "The proper way to judge a piece of jewelry is to feel it against your skin."

Of course, I was embarrassed. Had he asked me at the outset to place a crown upon his head, it is likely that I would have demurred, but now, seeing his second request as a politic way to evade his first, I acquiesced.

"Yes, of course," I said. "Touch is very important."

He bent forward, and I fastened the crown to his temples. It was elaborate, standing high above his head and adorned with feathers and semiprecious gems. It had two side panels that depended from the larger corona, and I righted those broad, beaded panels, laying them flat against his chest. Then I stepped back to allow him to look at himself.

The beauty of the piece transferred to Mr. Thibideaux. It bestowed an unusual quality to his form, which up until this moment had been quite ugly, almost obscene. Beneath the headpiece, Mr. Thibideaux's ugliness, while not departed, was somehow changed, so that I noticed less his decay and his filth, his foul posture and his stink, and more the brilliance of his unusual form—and how curious it was to see such brilliance drawing such ugly and intricate shapes. Difficult to describe; it was as though the visual plane, the whole world—Mr. Thibideaux—were made of tiny points of light.

The two of us had a nice discussion. He just left the headpiece on, like it was his own, and talked to me about different things. He said he was taking a vacation, and I said good for you. He asked if I knew of a place where he could buy a certain Japanese delicacy, and I told him that I had never heard of that delicacy. He said it was mostly eaten in the country, and I told him that my family has been metropolitan for many centuries.

"Come from samurai."

"Samurai," he said, "so then, like me, you are already dead."

I understood his reference to the *Hagakure*, of course. For reasons I can't name, the world inverted and I stood in a waking dream, Mr. Thibideaux himself a phantom.

"Don't I look . . ." Mr. Thibideaux craned his neck to see himself in the mirror behind me. He had trouble finding the word, but I could tell from his tone of voice that he was making a joke, so I pretended to laugh, and I was surprised to see color come into his cheeks.

He removed the headpiece and said, "I've come today to ask you about a commission."

"Actually, I'm sales manager, so mine is a salaried position."

"I wanted to know if it would be possible to order another bowl like the one I bought before."

"All Mr. Tatsusuke's bowls are one of a kind."

It took him a long time to explain what he wanted, which was a bowl like the one he bought before, in white, with the same gold inside. He wanted to order it as a commission, from Mr. Tatsusuke himself.

I told him we don't ordinarily do sales by commission, but he wouldn't take no for an answer, so I agreed to ask Mr. Seibu. That was probably not a wise decision.

Mr. Seibu and I have known each other a long time, and it's generally our habit to address one another in familiar forms of Japanese. That's why I didn't stand on ceremony but simply explained the situation. Actually, I was surprised by Mr. Seibu's response. He sat silently in his chair for a long time after I asked the question and didn't even ask me if I wanted to take a seat. He keeps his office in the traditional style, without a lot of clutter or noise, or any kind of telephone or computer to distract him from his duties as store president, so when he was quiet for so long, it felt like a form of rebuke. In fact, it certainly was a rebuke. I couldn't help fidgeting a little and trying to smooth my hair while he sat utterly still, with his hands folded on the slate-gray leather blotter before him.

More time passed. I began to think, Maybe he didn't under-

stand, so I started again, saying, "Mr. Seibu? We have a customer downsta—"

"I understand the question," he barked, and held up one
hand to tell me not to say it again.

"Of course, Mr. Seibu." I felt myself nodding; also, I realized I'd slipped into formal address. I thought, Okay, this
time I'm going to wait until he speaks.

After some time, Mr. Seibu took a deep breath and said,
"Fumi, let me ask you a question—have a seat."

"Yes, sir, thank you." I took a seat in one of his leather
chairs, and he said, "Fumi, I consider you a friend, and so I'm
going to speak to you as a friend."

"Thank you, sir."

"I'm very happy with your work on the floor, and I'm
very happy with your administrative abilities in overseeing
employees. All in all, your work has proved more than satis-
factory."

"Thank you, sir."

"However, I see room for improvement in your . . ." He
paused to seek the word and ultimately chose the English
phrase "self-confidence."

"Sir?"

"I don't mean to suggest that your mannerisms betray
any self-doubt," he said, and at that, I felt an insult in the
reference, however slight, to my fidgeting. "No, it is not a
matter of presentation, but rather that I've observed in you
some reluctance to take charge on the floor and make your
own decisions. Do you understand?"

Actually, I did not understand. I figured out later what

he meant, but at the time, I was shaken, and so I had a hard time seeing how this connected to the original question of the commission. What I thought at the time was, I have Mr. Thibideaux standing on the floor and likely causing some disruption, so I have to steer Mr. Seibu back to the original question, and then we can discuss this matter about my managerial style at a more appropriate time. I said, "Mr. Seibu, thank you. I will certainly evaluate my managerial . . ." Here I had trouble finding the word, and so after struggling a bit, I switched tack and said, "I'll put this criticism into use."

"It's not a criticism, Fumi."

"Naturally."

When I said that, he looked irritated, and I could tell he was thinking, First she says it's a criticism, then she says she knows it's not a criticism. I didn't know quite what to say, or why Mr. Seibu was so angry, so I said, "For the moment, however, maybe we can return to the original matter."

Mr. Seibu's nose turned purple. He has a problem with his heart, as well as unusually high blood pressure, with a high risk of stroke, so in moments like this, I worry that he will just explode and die. He said, "And what matter is that?"

"The small matter," I said, "of the bowl, and this commission a customer has—"

This time he really flew through the ceiling. He said, "That's up to you. That's up to you to make your own decision. That's up to you, Fumi. That's up to you as manager." I thanked him, and he said, "It's up to you to make your own decision. That's a decision for the sales manager."

He was still repeating this refrain as I eased his door closed.

I know Mr. Seibu too well. He and my husband were friends before the untimely passing, and while Mr. Seibu is unfailingly polite to me, I can remember in the old days he would have something to drink and say about such-and-such employee, "Oh, he doesn't know his ass from his elbow."

I placed a call to Mr. Tatsusuke. He remembered me right away, and he asked after my son. I told him he was doing very well, and I thanked him for the gift he sent him on his wedding day. Then I told him the situation, and he did not hesitate to agree to the commission. "Anything for you, Fumi. If you ask it, I have no choice but to say yes. Yes, a white bowl for Fumi." He didn't even charge extra for the special request.

When I explained everything to Mr. Thibideaux, he didn't hesitate. "Fantastic," he said, and while I was ringing his deposit, he explained that the second bowl was also for his guru. I didn't want to say anything, but somehow found myself saying, "He's going to have a lot of bowls."

Mr. Thibideaux didn't have an answer for that, so I asked if he studied Buddhism in Japan.

"Study?" he said. "I lived six weeks in a *zendo*. I never would have left, but my mother is ill."

Then he started to talk to me about his problems. Actually, this is something a lot of Western customers will do; we even receive training for it. It is best, when the customers do this, to seem neither embarrassed nor sympathetic. If you seem embarrassed, then the customer will realize he has been impolite. If you pretend to feel sympathy, the customer can sense your deception. And if you actually feel sympathy, then that is likely to create an unprofessional situation. I put my hands together, palms straight, just in front of my body and lowered my eyes.

However, Mr. Thibideaux's credit-card charge was stuck in the machine, so while he spoke and I held my position, I worried that his $100 deposit was going to be declined. All this time he was explaining to me that his mother was suffering from syphilis, the sex disease. He said the two of them shared an apartment on the water, and then he started to talk about the great flood of 1992, and the mildew in the carpet.

I picked up the card machine and shook it. I looked to make sure the plugs had not come undone. Maybe that didn't make sense to do, because the screen was all lit up. Then three beeps sounded, and the receipts came out the machine's end.

"Can I just get you to sign here, please?"

Once Mr. Thibideaux had signed, I said, "And that'll be it."

I handed him his copy of the receipt, smiled, and bowed. He stood there, searching my eyes.

I said, "The white is going to be beautiful with the gold."

"Or it's going to look like an Ed Gein."

I didn't understand the reference.

"John Gotti," he corrected himself. "You know, a mafioso."

I blinked.

"Didn't you ever see those movies?"

"Right." I made my fake laugh, but the color in his cheeks did not brighten, and he did not smile.

When the bowl came in, I understood what Mr. Thibideaux meant about John Gotti. The white and the gold were sumptuous in a way that American filmmakers associate with the high life of a mafioso. I don't mean to say that the bowl was ugly—in fact, it was striking in its beauty—but rather, that it took seeing the bowl to understand what it was Mr. Thibideux had tried to express.

Ordinarily, I am efficient in the dispatch of my duties, but in the matter of the Tatsusuke commission, I found myself procrastinating. I was reluctant to call Mr. Thibideaux. Sometimes I would begin to make the call, and then I would remember some other pressing matter. Other times, I sat for a long time in front of the phone, unable to pick it up and dial the numbers. I understand this is quite ordinary for others, but for me, this behavior is highly unusual. I also found myself lingering around the bowl, staring into it for long stretches of time.

I put a small white label on Mr. Thibideaux's bowl, and handwrote on that label the word "sold." I did not place the bowl out, where an unscrupulous customer could unpeel the label, but rather used it in a jewelry display. I placed it, perhaps a bit contrary to Mr. Tatsusuke's wish, in one of our jewel-box street displays, adjacent to a very precious item made of twisted settings of uncut ruby stones.

The bowl did not go unremarked. The white Mr. Tatsu-suke had chosen for the tea bowl was stainless. It was subtly luminous, and offset by the gold, it was luxurious. Unlike many potters who imitate the work of Lucie Rie, Mr. Tatsu-suke does not aspire to ever-increasing feats of thinness in his clay, nor is he interested in a smooth exterior and flawless lines—a yoga student's idea of peace. Mr. Tatsusuke's hand is bold. He has a masculine commitment to his imperfections, rather than a fretting quality. His craftsmanship is masterly, and this particular bowl stood out from the body of his work. It was like a declaration of love. For what, I was unsure.

It was a month later, sometime in the middle of a weekday afternoon, that Mrs. Thibideaux and I had our only conversa-tion. I had let the phone ring and ring, so I was startled when the rings came to a halt, and after a little fumbling, a woman spoke to me with great confusion.

"Hello?" she said. "Hello?"

"Good afternoon," I said. "I hope I didn't wake you?"

She just gave a cough and then apologized for her cough.

I said, "No need to apologize. I'm calling from Seibu de-partment store. I was calling to inform Gerard Thibideaux that his commission has arrived in the store."

"Hello?"

"Yes, good afternoon, I'm calling from Seibu downtown. Is Gerard Thibideaux available?"

"Jerry?"

"Yes, he had ordered a bowl from us, and I wanted to in-form him it has come in the store."

"Jerry isn't here!"

"All right, could you please inform him—"

I heard her fumbling the phone in its cradle, and after a few moments, she managed to hang up.

My shyness about the bowl began to diminish. As days became weeks, I got in the habit of calling regularly. I think it was about twenty-one days later when, abruptly, Mr. Thibideaux answered the phone.

"Thibideaux residence, Jerry speaking."

"Mr. Thibideaux, this is Fumi at Seibu department store."

"Hello, Fumi. How are you?"

"Yes, I'm fine. I was calling to inform you that your commission has arrived in the store."

"Uh-huh, thank you, Fumi. I appreciate that."

"Of course. Do you know when you might be free to come in?"

"No, Fumi—to be honest, I don't."

"Sir? The bowl is in the store, for clarification. It has already arrived in the store. That's for clarification purposes."

He started to say something, but then he stopped, and for a little bit of time, both of us were quiet.

"Mr. Thibideaux?"

"Yes?"

"Your bowl has come into the store four or five weeks ago. Do you know—"

"I heard that, Fumi."

"Oh."

Then we were quiet again.

"Mr. Thibideaux," I said, but before I could continue he said, "I'm waiting for some cash to land. Fumi, I'm waiting for some cash to land in my account."

He began to tell me something about check number 622. I said, "Perhaps you could make a payment." Then he started to tell me about a trust fund in Mississippi. He explained his great-grandfather was a pine baron. He talked about caring for his mother, about how much it cost him, and then his mother began to shout at him in the background. Actually, she was quite capable of saying things that were unkind. Mr. Thibideaux said, "Fumi, would it be all right if I called you back?"

But rather than letting me answer, he just hung up the phone.

Months passed with no word from Mr. Thibideaux. He never called, and he never answered the phone when I called. I left messages. I even considered writing him a card. I thought about it quite often. Once, I even found myself thinking about it under the strange conditions of a dream. I was trying to get some nails and tacks gathered in crumpled-up newspaper while at sea, in an old wooden sailboat, amid tossing white-crested waves. I was in the bottom of the boat, in a small cellar, so the tossing waves caused the nails to keep escaping my grasp. "It doesn't matter," somebody was telling me, and I was saying, "No, it does matter. It matters a lot!"

It was a small thing, an inconvenience, but it grew in my mind, so that when I looked at, when I even thought about,

Mr. Thibideaux's bowl, I felt sick to my stomach. It became the kind of incident a person could explain to a psychologist.

Several days after Mr. Tatsusuke died of natural causes, Mr. Seibu asked me to show him the white bowl from the jewel-box display. It had been a year since I had spoken on the phone with Mr. Thibideaux. Mr. Seibu ran his fingers along the spiral divot inside the bowl, where Tatsusuke had traced his fingers through the clay. He turned the bowl to examine its bottom, and I knew he wanted to take it. This is quite ordinary for Mr. Seibu, who could of course have any item in his store.

I knew he was going to take the bowl. I also knew that I was going to have a telephone call from Mr. Thibideaux. What I did not know was that Mr. Thibideaux was going to choose that particular moment to appear in the store, like the fox. He stood behind Mr. Seibu, who was saying, yes, maybe he would like to take the bowl to his home.

I nodded. I took the bowl and turned. I began to wrap it in tissue paper, and then I stopped. It was my responsibility to explain that the bowl belonged to Mr. Thibideaux. I took a moment to compose my words.

"Fumi"—Mr. Seibu gave me a funny look and extended his open palm to take the bowl. He bowed and said good night.

Actually, Mr. Thibideaux never spoke. He just turned and walked out slowly, even stopping to pick up a Daum figurine of a penguin. I considered racing out onto the sidewalk and taking Mr. Seibu by his sleeve. I would just have to explain—it was a commission, I made a mistake. But I was uncertain, thinking of all the different ways to begin.

Later that week, I received an envelope, and inside it I found a card. On the front of the card was a photograph of a naked old man who was tied to the ceiling by ropes and had some kind of foam smeared all around his bottom. A second old man, wearing a lot of leather, had his fist inside the first man's bottom. I probably should have just thrown the card away, but I opened it and found a long inscription in a delicate hand.

Mr. Thibideaux wrote that he understood what had happened and bore me no ill will. He explained that he hated this world and everyone in it. The people whom he had once considered friends had abandoned him when his father died and his money was spent, and his mother had contracted this disease. He told me he himself had AIDS, and he described the circumstances under which he had contracted it. He said there is nothing beautiful in this world, nothing wholesome, and nothing sane. He said people everywhere are like figures in a certain painting by Bosch, and the time he spent in monasteries was characterized by impassioned bickering over the smallest things—the sound of chewing, the way a certain man moved his fingers. He told me how they fired an old cook just because he was flatulent, and because he used too much salt. When you drink a cup of tea, he said, you are a party to misery, and then I stopped reading what he had to say.

I never mentioned Mr. Thibideaux's card to anyone. I imagine that he hoped to disturb me, sending that kind of card, but I am not some flower. I have been alive for more than fifty years, and I have thought many ugly things. Miserable people often think they have a special purchase on the truth. My husband was one of those. At the moment of his death, I told him I was relieved. He gasped, and then everything was torn away.

Catholic

In the morning, I wrote an email to this priest I knew. It had been a long time since I'd thought of him. I told him that I had spent the weekend with a guy I met on a plane. "But I guess I am too intense, or something." I asked him if I could stay in his place in Paris. I said, "I know this is a lot to ask, but I feel very lonely right now, and like you are the only person I can say these things to."

He answered immediately: "I won't be checking email for the next month or so." It took me a second to realize that it was an autoreply message.

The next morning he wrote: "Don't worry. I think you will meet other boys. Be flamboyant. I don't have a place in Paris. I used to have one in London."

At my job, I had a desk that looked out at the tar-painted second-story roof where people from the music department went to smoke. I went out there to call the plane guy. I walked back and forth on a wooden board, and then squatted down and rested on my calves. I told the plane guy I never wanted to talk to him again. He said that was childish.

My friend Lee asked me to see a movie. We agreed to meet at a German restaurant around the corner from the theater.

Lee and I were not close friends. We had met about ten years before. At that time Lee was a computer programmer. He was also in a band. He was having a touch of success when I first met him, which made my close friend—whom Lee dated—angry. She said, "I have known a thousand bands who were supposedly about to blow up, and it never happens." She was frightened that she would lose Lee, or that he would have all the power in their relationship. Lee did become famous, but he always loved my friend, and in the end it was much more complicated between them.

By this time, by the time we met at the German restaurant, my friend had broken up with Lee, and was dating Bill Clinton's young press advisor. Lee'd had some real success and he was at the beginning of his decline. He knew it was the beginning of his decline, and so did everyone around him, but he tried not to accept it.

Lee and I were still friends for one reason: we often saw each other at Starbucks. We were the only people like us who went to Starbucks. At first we ignored each other. I would have been okay to leave it that way, but Lee was a descendant of John Singer Sargent, so he had excellent manners. He came up to my table one day and said, "Hi." After that we'd sit together with our laptops when we saw each other. We had almost nothing to say.

I got to the German place an hour early. The restaurant was empty except for a guy at the bar. He was a little chubby. I could tell he was single because he was wearing white tube socks with black dress shoes. His jeans were too tight on him. I don't mean that he had on skinny jeans, I mean that he had on jeans that were two sizes too small, and he was uncomfortable. He kept squirming, fooling with his phone.

There was something in the air. I don't understand how it works. Everything looked brighter.

I was happy to be distracted from the guy on the plane. I had called him a couple times, after telling him I didn't want to speak to him again, but he hadn't answered. I was waiting for the bartender to see me. Outside, through the window, I saw an old guy stop under a tree, pull down a branch, and smell a flower. The chubby guy at the bar was looking at his phone. The bartender was on his knees, wiping something with a towel. The priest was unusual. He had told me, "Forget AA. Forget being sober. Address your emotional life and none of that is necessary." I was four months sober. I didn't know what was right—whether I should drink or be sober. I wasn't into religion, but after the weekend with the guy from the airplane—a weekend I don't know how to explain—I wanted to believe in something. The plane guy and I took hallucinogens together, as well as painkillers, and maybe the drugs made me insane, because I could almost hear the priest urging me to order a drink.

The bartender got up off the ground and came over to where I was sitting. He threw a coaster down and looked at me. I had trouble getting the words out, but I ordered a vodka martini.

"What kind of vodka?"

"Just Stolichnaya, or Stoli, or whatever."

"Stoli."

"Yes, Stoli. Or whatever."

When Lee showed up, I was having my second martini.

"I'm drinking," I said.

"That's fine."

"I haven't had a drink in four months, but I don't care."

"That's fine." He sat beside me and ordered a beer. "How do you like it?"

"I like it," I said.

He looked embarrassed for me. We were quiet. I didn't want to go to the movie. Lee drank a beer, and we tossed a coin, and we ended up going to another bar.

I opened the door to the second bar, and a guy swung around. He had been leaning against the door, so when I opened it, his face was only a few inches from mine. I remember his teeth. He had a canine that came out at the side, and his front teeth were fine and white and flat. He had a messy beard, and he wore glasses that magnified his hazel eyes. He was striking. He had his palms against either side of a pint glass of beer. It was like the figure holding a lantern on the cover of *Stairway to Heaven*, or Rasputin. He was tall and square-shouldered. He wore an army jacket with the sleeves rolled, and something about him looked religious. I mean, he looked like Jesus.

"I didn't know you were back yet," Lee said.

"We got back last night." The guy stepped back to let us in.

"How was it?"

"Ah, you know."

They talked a little more like that. Then Lee remembered I was there. He said, "You guys've met, right?"

"I know I know you," the guy said. "Where is it that I know you from?"

"I'm not sure," I said. "You look kind of familiar."

I knew who he was. He was the drummer from Catholic. We had met the previous Christmas, at the same bar, but only for a little while. He was married to the singer in his band. The singer was an interesting woman. She had long, frizzy, curly blond hair and she had a tummy. She wore tight Lycra skirts with low cheap heels and strange T-shirts that looked like they came from Units. She wrote good lyrics. She didn't seem like she loved the drummer anymore. He said, "Oh yeah, wait a second. I know exactly who you are! You're that writer girl."

"Well, sort of."

"No." He looked at me with a funny smile. He had his mouth closed, twisted a little to the side, like he was hiding it. "You are."

"I'm going to get a drink."

The bar was crowded. People were standing two or three deep behind the chairs. Waiting to get through gave me time to relax. I drank a drink standing there and got another one and went back to him and Lee.

He invited us to come hang out with him in back. He and I got caught up in the crowd and we let Lee go ahead.

He asked me what music I liked.

"I don't really know any music. I just sort of go on song jags where I listen to the same song over and over again."

"What?"

I repeated it, and he said, "What bands do you listen to over and over again?"

"I like that Arthur Lee band Love."

"What?"

"That Arthur Lee band Love."

He nodded, and his eyes and cheeks swelled up a little. He showed a lot on his face. He said, "Who else?"

"I like your guys' band."

He swelled up more. His face turned red. I was happy that he was still vulnerable enough that he could be flattered. I said, "What movies do you like?"

"*Sophie's Choice*. With Meryl Streep?"

"I've never seen that, but my friend Zbigniew says the book's really good."

"The book is garbage."

"Zbigniew has pretty good taste. He said the language is beautiful in it."

"The book," he said again, "is garbage."

"Well, I'll look for the movie."

He asked me what I did, and I said, "I'm an editor at a magazine. Actually, maybe you could write for us."

This was my old trick.

"Do you have like a card?" he said.

"No."

"Here." He reached out and touched the arm of the girl beside him. He said, "Do you have a card?" The girl handed him a card. He started to write his phone number down.

"Don't give me your number!"

He looked startled.

I said, "I hate the phone."

"It's just for texts." He crossed his number out and said, "Fine." He wrote his email down on the card.

A few hours later, in the booth where we were all sitting, the drummer elbowed my ribs and whispered in my ear. "Just talk to me."

"What?"

He whispered with a hand over his mouth, "Come over here and just talk to me."

We got into a different booth. He said, "She was doing a metafeminist critique on you," and he glanced at a girl we'd left. She was at the other booth. She was about my age, maybe a couple years older. She was friends with him and with his wife.

I was drunk and I can't remember what we talked about. We talked for a long time. When the bar closed, the three of us—the drummer, Lee, and I—went to Lee's house. Actually, we made a stop at the drummer's house first. He was blacked out, I think. He was repeating himself. As we drove up to his house, he kept asking if we wanted "coke or X." When he came back with the Ecstasy he kept saying, "You only need half. Half is good." He put half in my mouth and kissed me. Up close his white pocked cheek was like brushing the surface of the moon.

When we got to Lee's, the drummer and I went into Lee's bedroom. I realized Lee was coming, too. I stopped in the doorway and waited a second. Lee understood. He turned back, and passed out on his couch. The drummer and I took Lee's bed. I was seeing white pills, like television static moving evenly across the blue field of my vision. He went to close the door and came back to where I was kneeling on the bed. I reached a hand up to touch his face. Then I took off his pants. I thought he had a very small penis. I tried to get him hard.

He said, "I'm sorry, it's just not."

I stopped what I was doing. "Sorry."

"No, it's just. Sometimes it's just not."

He got me onto my back and went down on me, but I couldn't feel anything because I was drunk. I tapped his shoulder, and he came up.

He said, "Called up."

"It isn't that."

"Sure."

"No, it isn't."

When we woke up in the morning, he checked his phone. He switched it off and said, "That's it. We're divorced. I'm going to be sleeping in a ditch."

I was sitting on the side of the bed, buckling my shoe. He said, "Wait." I turned and looked at him. He said, "Let me see your underwear again." I flipped my skirt up. I believed he wanted something to jerk off to when I left. I got up and put my back against Lee's wall, facing him, and slid along it toward the door, watching him.

He said, "Wait, let me get your number or something."

"You already have it," I said. It was a lie.

"Really?"

"Yeah."
"Okay."
"Okay."

I had my computer on my lap in the back room of Starbucks. I got an email in my junk mail saying that I had a message from Wartime82. I figured it was some Third World salesman, but I was bored and so I logged on to read it. The subject heading of the message was "Sleuth." In the body the drummer wrote: "Hey, found you here. I'm in London right now, sleeping off a Xanax buzz. La-la-la, one of the summer crowd, taking pleasure in the English sun. I hope this day brings you many pleasant moments."

I wrote him back, describing my shoes, which I had gotten free at work. I said I'd asked my coworker about them, and he'd become grave, looked me in the eye, and said, "They're cool."

I need to tell you I was crazy. I was crazy at the time.

After about ten days, I wrote to him again. I described the pit bulls that were up for adoption on my street, how they were leashed to the iron poles of the scaffolding, like a gauntlet of wild dogs, and how each one wore an orange vest that said, "Adopt me."

He wrote back: "I'm here at Radio France HQ and a Frenchman, wearing a pirate-y-looking shirt, is pulling me away from the computer. Bye for now."

·

My psychiatrist was an overweight woman who specialized in eating disorders. She worked out of the bedroom of a ground-floor Union Square apartment. The bedroom had one window on the floor of the windshaft. It got a diffused gray light. She had Victorian figurines on her bookshelves, and a bunch of books about food. They took different approaches—scientific, clinical, mystical, experiential. She also had baskets of toys on the floor and on the dirty velvet couch.

At the beginning of each meeting I had to fill out a form. One of the questions was "Have you been having any strange thoughts?"

I always wrote, "No."

She had monochrome auburn hair and wore turtlenecks under unbuttoned shirts. She was always asking me if I did late-night snacking. I had the impression that she was convinced I snacked at night. Sometimes I would get frustrated and say, "Do you mean, have I ever eaten after dark?" I would force her to explain she meant waking up in the middle of the night and going to the refrigerator half asleep to eat. "No, I don't do that." She'd make a note and, the next time we saw each other, ask the question again. She kept her patient files piled on her desk. She had them piled uniformly about a foot and a half high, so she created a writing surface out of them, but she had to raise her arms to write.

She recommended some medication. She described the pill she recommended. She said it was known to cause weight loss, a side effect. I was open to that. She warned that it had some unusual side effects, including word loss and lethargy. I thought that would be all right. She advised me to let her know if I experienced anything more unusual than that.

That night I wrote to the priest. "You were right. I met another one. He likes me, I think, but I am afraid he will tear me apart."

He wrote: "Of course he will. Being torn apart is what a relationship is. So don't be afraid. Play the game."

I met one of my friends for dinner, and we walked to a bar. The leaves were making a dry clicking sound. They were gray in the streetlight, and moving with the wind, which was changing direction, making the leaves look like schools of fish. I saw the drummer coming toward me and my friend. He was talking on his cell phone. I bent forward at the waist to catch his eye, and he frowned. As we came closer, I noticed that he was gasping for air and dripping with sweat. He extended his hand like an iron rail at my friend, and he said in a loud, manly voice, "I'm Elliot."

My friend mumbled his name.

I said, "Are you late or something?"

The drummer said, "Yes. Do you know where the Tea Lounge is? The Tea Lounge?"

My friend pointed it out, and the drummer crossed the street at a diagonal. He ran to get away from us. I asked my friend what he thought of it, after about a block, and he said, "Nothin'."

When I got home I described it all to the priest. He wrote back, "COME ON you are thinking too much."

I wrote: "I love him. I think maybe he loves me. Please tell me."

The next afternoon at Starbucks I got his answer: "Yes, he does, but he is afraid."

I stood up and went walking on the street. I hugged my computer to my chest. I had walked about a block when I realized that the priest didn't know how the drummer felt.

I was at a sushi restaurant. The sushi chef was missing the tip of his pointer finger. It was recent and looked like he'd cut it three-quarters off and just torn off the tip and gone back to work. I watched him slicing salmon. I ordered another small pitcher of sake.

I wrote to the priest on my phone: "I thought maybe I should just tell him how I feel. I thought maybe I should even just email it."

He wrote back: "Yes, say it."

I tried, but I couldn't do it. Writing "I" into the message body field made me shake violently. I wrote: "I was wondering if you could come over sometime," and sent that.

A fat businessman started up a conversation with me about fresh wasabi. Then I wrote to the priest. I said, "I can't. Is that enough? There's time, isn't there?"

That night around 2 a.m. I woke up to the sound of thunder. Half sleeping, I thought God was communicating with me through the weather. I said, "Not now. Not now." The thunder redoubled.

I sat up in bed and waited. After a few minutes I went to the window. The sky was full of light. Missiles were falling to the ground. I envisioned a brief, bleak, postapocalyptic future—wolves, yellow light, rags. I really believed that I was going to die, and then my mind went to the drummer, and I was sorry I hadn't told him how I felt. It wasn't because it mattered. It was because it didn't matter.

I went outside, and then I could tell it was a storm. It was a summer storm, heat lightning, and the lightning was that strange kind that comes in plumes. I'd mistaken it for missiles. So I wrote an email to the drummer. "I woke up to the sound of thunder. I went to the window and thought the lightning was missiles. I thought I was going to die, and I felt sad I never told you that I love you. I came outside and it was clearly a storm. A homeless man who looked like Bob Marley was running down the street. He stopped in front of me, did a jig, held up two peace signs and ran."

The drummer came to my apartment a month later. He held his palm to his chest, bent over. He rested with his hands on his knees in the doorway. Then he started taking off his shoes. He said, "Do you have any water?"

"You don't have to take your shoes off," I said.

"I always take my shoes off."

After he had taken his shoes off, he sat against the wall with his knees folded into his chest and his arms wrapped around them.

I got up and opened the oven. I tapped the quiche, took it out, and cut two pieces. When we had eaten, the drummer said, "I would have a second piece, but I'm on the baseball diet. You don't have to clean your plate, but then, every night, like clockwork, you have a scoop of vanilla ice cream."

"I don't have ice cream. Anyway, you don't need to lose weight."

"For a while I was getting a little heavy. I was turning into one of those skinny guys with a potbelly."

"I think that's kind of cute," I said. He frowned, so I said, "But you don't have to."

I brought the plates into the kitchen. We went outside and sat on my steps. The drummer asked me what a normal week was like, and I didn't know how to say, "I'm alone all the time." I had it in my head that his life was full of glamour. I said something about work and friends.

"That sounds nice," he said.

"Yeah, it's okay."

He told me about being in Dallas. He said their waitress drew a diagram to show the path of the bullet that shot Kennedy in the head. He wasn't a very good storyteller, and I could see he was trying to say there was some kind of magic in the moment, but to me it just sounded like a thing a waitress told people.

"I can't explain it," he said, noticing my expression. "Having all this shown to you by a Texas girl."

I said, "I'm from Texas."

I told a story about my aunt. She had been in the Bolshoi Ballet, and then she got a degree in quantum mechanics from Rice. Then she tried to run her husband over in a parking lot, and she was fired, and years went by, and she was arrested for disorderly conduct in Houston. She was in the drunk tank with her boyfriend and my mom picked her up. When she came out, she said, "Patty, I think that police officer raped me," and her boyfriend, who was still in the tank, cupped his hands around his mouth and yelled, "Both of 'em did, baby."

I laughed at the story, but I could tell it made the drummer uneasy. He asked me if I had any history of mania in my family, and I said, "Well, obviously, her." I was pretty sure he was leading us toward a so-called healthy discussion about the end of our communication, so I was surprised when he said, "What should we do now?"

"I don't know."

"We could go out."

"Do you want to?"

"Well, do you have any *wine*?"

"I do. I didn't bring it out with dinner because I thought you didn't drink."

"Ha, right."

"You asked for water."

"I was thirsty."

We went into the kitchen. I held up a cut-crystal glass with a stem and a simple crystal sake glass.

"For wine? I think that one." He pointed to the one with the stem. "It's more *elegant*." He laid emphasis on the word "elegant" in the uncomfortable way that he did with words he liked.

He had a sip of wine and I handed him a fig. He took my hand and said, "Let me see your nails." There was purple fig peel under two nails. He thought it was dirt and he grimaced. Then he gave me my hand back and looked into my eyes for a long time.

"So . . . what else can we talk about?" he said.

"I don't know. I don't mind being quiet with people. Do you?"

"No."

We started talking again. We sat on the floor in front of the bay window. It was summer, and the sun set late. The drummer said that, in Europe, his brother had gone through customs with marijuana in his carry-on.

"Why?"

"He said he forgot it was there. I told him that was so stupid. I don't know. I think he just wanted it."

We were quiet. I looked at the open windows. I said, "Do you think people can hear us?"

"Who?"

"Well, the windows are open."

"No one can hear us. My voice is incredibly soft."

"Mine, too."

"I have the world's softest voice."

"No, I do."

I stood up to get the wine, and he said, "You're so attractive to me. Does everyone think so?"

I wanted to say no, but instead I just looked at him.

He said, "I bet weird guys fall at your feet."

I said, "I have one beer in the fridge. We can share it." I came back to sit with him. He said, "Can I touch your legs?" He was sitting Indian-style, and I put my legs between his knee and arm. He put both hands on me and said, "I feel guilty."

"Why?"

"Well, you know I'm married."

"I think you'll always be married."

"I love her."

I sat on top of him. Without thinking about how you do it, I mean, without thinking about how other people do it, I touched him.

"Can you take my shorts off?" I said.

He took them off. I had a dress tucked into them. It came to my mid-thighs. He said, "What's this?"

"Some weird— It was an impulse buy. It's from India."

What happened next was languorous and slow. We were like cats. We got into my bed. The drummer was lying on his back, and I was sitting on his lap with my knees bent. I leaned back and lay on his shins, and took his feet in my hands.

"You have a wet spot," he said. "Is that from arousal?"

I lifted myself up and lay on top of him. I said, "Have you done this before?"

He went back on tour the next morning. He drove to Canada. He texted me a few nights later. I was already asleep, and I woke up to a string of them. In the first he was describing the people outside the venue when his show was over—a man in a Corvette and a streetwalker. Then later he wrote: "Everything comes crashing down in the back of a cab in Toronto listening to stupid jazz." I knew it didn't mean anything, but at the same time, I thought it meant his wife was pregnant and I'd never see him again. I wrote: "What do you mean?" A few days later he answered, "Ignore last text."

From Canada he went to Europe, on a tour that ended in Russia. I can remember that I came undone, but not how or why. I wrote too often. Once, when he was in France, I woke up and he had answered twenty of my emails. It was strange. I was relieved. On the subway into work, I fell out of love, like I was the one who was being smothered. And by noon, I was terrified that I would lose him.

I went to lunch alone and drank. I came back from lunch and wrote to the drummer. I wrote, "This isn't working," and he wrote back immediately, "Okay you're right." Then for years, mostly what I did was email him, and try not to email him. I would count the days, and sometimes make it to a week. I would get drunk and text-message him about my mystical experiences and my homeless friends. He wrote me to describe a bar in Russia with shrines to Lenin and murals of Putin doing karate. He said the street dogs knew their stops, and he met a guy from a magazine who could not drink because he had been bitten by a rabid dog, and he was taking "dog pills." When he got home, sometimes he would call me. It was always when he was blacked out and I was asleep. I never caught the calls. I then sent him a long email about the acorn lady and her barren three-million-dollar apartment. I described lawyers I overheard, monkeys I saw. Other drummers I had sex with. I told him a tree of plum blossoms fell on me and I saw some young men wearing outfits. I described the man at the wine store. I always wish there was a point to all those emails. Maybe there was. I don't know. I do know. There was.

Finally I went to see his band perform live. By that time they were famous. My stepdaughters owned his albums. Before they played a song with the refrain "my head is wrong," he seemed to get my eye. That was the last time we looked at each other.

Mynahs

"Last year, the visiting teachers got up and said something about themselves."

"That was because you were all new," Greer said. "You'd just gotten here."

"But I don't know who they are, I mean." The student looked at Donald Burdon.

"Well, why not. Professor Burdon? Would you mind?"

Donald started. He was shivering and sweating. It was the middle of January, but he didn't have an overcoat.

"Maybe you could say a little bit about your workshop?" Greer said helpfully.

"I'm going to do the ordinary thing."

"Maybe you could turn and face them?"

Professor Burdon jerked up halfway out of his chair.

"I'm going to do the ordinary thing," he said. "It's going to be a workshop. I won't deviate from the norm, of what you've come to expect."

Professor Burdon sat down.

"Thank you, Professor Burdon," Greer said. "What about you, Guillermo?"

Guillermo Silva stood decorously and made eye contact with the MFA students. He said, "My first instinct is to tell you to take workshop with Donald here. In fact, I'm going to teach Donald's memoir in the spring. But you'll think I'm being a lazy professor if I don't encourage you to join my class. So, let's see. I'm from the South, so I favor courtesy. I tend to like to work on novel excerpts for reasons I won't get into right now. Beyond that, what can I say? You're all here because you're good. My hope is to help you write *the* story."

Professor Burdon shot his cuffs. It sounded like he said, "Cocksucker."

Donald Burdon and Benjamin Greer had met two decades earlier, in John Berryman's poetry workshop. It was a two-year program, but Donald was in his fifth year, because he'd had to leave several times.

Berryman asked his twelve students to show up on the first day with an unsigned, typewritten poem. He collected the pages, shuffled them, and passed them around. Then the students went in a circle, reading one another's work.

Greer's poem was read third. It was the first time he heard his work read by somebody else. He realized, after a few words, that his poem was purple. It was self-aggrandizing. It pandered to John Berryman. But he wondered if it just seemed that way in the context of all these other student poems. He regretted his decision to get an MFA. "Poet school," he murmured.

After the break, when each anonymous poem had been read, Berryman spoke a little. He asked the students what they thought of the experience, and said, "It's easier to be honest when a piece is unsigned. Of course, there are some things we can never say, because they are secrets, but we can show our hearts."

The students went in a circle praising lines and images from one another's poems. When it was his turn, Greer looked squarely at Berryman and praised a prose poem about two Jewish men sharing a cup of tea. He said, "I love the image it evokes."

Berryman said, "Really?"

"Yes, you know. How those little things will matter. It's really rather extraordinary."

"To me it seemed clichéd."

"The cliché makes it extraordinary."

Berryman raised his eyebrows. "Say more."

Greer swallowed. "Often, when he is . . . worried . . . a man . . . a bearded man, will, you know, sort of scrape his hands through his beard."

Berryman looked around at the other students. "Hm."

The classroom door swung open, cracking against the wall. Donald Burdon stood in the doorway. He was drenched with sweat. He wore golfing shorts that were too small. He said, "I am so sorry," and began to pass out one typewritten page to each student. It was his poem.

"I'm sorry I'm late," he said as he gave a page to Greer.

"I'm dreadfully sorry. Please, bear with me. Mr. Berryman, please accept my sincerest apology. Please bear with me. Accept my sincere apology."

Greer looked down at the page Donald had given him. The poem began, "She dropped to all four paws, stood still and looked at me."

It was a poem about losing his virginity. Donald had slept with an older woman when they were driving her car to Colorado. She made him wait to penetrate her until the numbers on the odometer rolled over from 99,999 to zeros. It was a good poem.

Donald was still explaining why he was late with his poem. It was due to his living situation, which sounded complicated.

"Why'd you move in?" Berryman asked. He was sympathetic.

"It's actually pretty nice. Plus it was the first listing that I saw," Donald said. "I've been having sort of a difficult time. We aren't all famous professors. Some of us have tax liens. I have a tax lien, from a speaking engagement I did three years ago. I regret accepting it. I had to pretend to be Chickasaw. I don't have any money to pay this lien, and now they're trying to take it from my mother, who happens to be dying in a hospital—and my father, well, if you'd read my poem at all, you'd know that he is a rapist."

After a moment, Berryman said, "Well. What else. What did you like, what didn't you?"

Donald took a seat. He raised his hand.

"Yes, fine, you," Berryman said, "no need to raise your hand."

"I didn't get a chance to read the poems."

"That's all right."

"I'd like the opportunity to participate."

"Next time."

"Please, Professor Berryman. Please. Let me participate."

Berryman asked the students to pass the poems to Donald, and he flipped through the pages with theatrical irritation. He appeared to be reading first lines. Then he came to a stop. He raised his hand.

"Yes, Mr. Burdon," Berryman said. "Go ahead."

Donald read Greer's poem aloud, from start to finish.

Later that week, Donald taught Greer about cocaine. He said, "To get it, and this is not something I tell you with pleasure, we will have to go into Brown Town. I know that it would be better if I had a dealer, but you see once one has a dealer one runs into the problem of becoming an addict, at least this way—watch your step."

Donald pointed to a pile of dog shit. He took Greer to a part of town Greer had never seen or heard of before. He was pretty sure no one knew about it, and he even wondered if perhaps it was a place that Donald had dreamed. It was a ghetto.

Donald stopped at a payphone and picked up the receiver. "Quit pacing! You look like a narc."

A few minutes later a man in a leather coat walked by. He had his hands in his pockets. Greer put his hands in his pockets.

"Come on," Donald said. He walked Greer around to the other side of the street. On the corner he handed a young woman money. They returned to the phone. Donald picked up the receiver. A few moments later, the man in the leather coat walked by again. This time, he spat at Donald's feet and said, "Be back, bitch."

Donald dove down and grabbed the small wad of tin foil. He took a cosmetic mirror out of his pocket and emptied the coke onto it. He sniffed half and passed the mirror to Greer. He said, "Come on." They went to Kenney's Bar, where they saw Berryman.

"Absolute fucking shit," he said.

"Mr. Berryman?"

"Go home. Get a fry cook. Thas a profeshun."

"May we join you?" Donald said. "May we buy you a drink?"

Berryman took a long drink, leaving beer foam in his beard. "You there in back!" he shouted. "Black man!"

Greer followed Berryman's gaze to a window to the kitchen, where a cook was making hamburgers. "Now thas a man. That black . . . guy. Monsieur Le Chef! Salud!" Berryman raised his glass and smiled, then began to sing along with the jukebox in a high, slushy voice. The cook ignored him.

Berryman tried to roll a cigarette. Most of the tobacco ended up on his hands and jacket. He smoothed his oily hair, then he padded his pockets in search of a lighter. The bartender slid one down the bar. Berryman didn't notice.

Donald Burdon picked up the lighter and held it before Berryman, who clasped Donald's hand and took his time.

Donald said, "Professor Berryman, may we join you?"

Berryman inhaled. He coughed and swallowed.

"Mr. Berryman?"

"Wha."

"May we join you?" Donald said. "May we buy you a drink?"

"You there!" Berryman shouted. "Black man!"

Greer started.

Berryman knocked over his beer.

"That's okay. That's okay," Berryman said. "I'm okay."

"A scotch," Donald said.

The bartender poured a scotch, and Donald placed it on a coaster before Berryman.

"A gentleman! Thank you, kind sir."

Berryman held up his glass. "You there! Black man. First sip for the chef!" He took a sip of scotch. "Now thas a man. That black . . . guy. Monsieur Le Chef!"

Berryman turned his head and looked at his students. After a few moments he recognized them. He put his arm around Donald and gave him a kiss on the cheek. "These are my students," he said to the bartender.

The bartender frowned. Berryman waved a dismissive hand at him. He turned back to Donald and Greer.

"New York City. Thas a lesson. Sit down with the editors. Then you'll get a lesson in cocksucking."

"Well, of course," Greer said. He sipped his beer. "But first I want to master the form."

Berryman caught himself on Greer's shoulder and left his hand there.

Greer said, "Mr. Berryman, writing isn't a choice I made. I mean, it just sort of happened. I guess I was lonely, and I didn't get along with people, and I was inspired by—or I was imitating—poems like yours. Then one thing led to another, and here I am."

Berryman laughed long, loud, and hard into Greer's face. He slapped a worn-out drunk beside him. The man had a long, red, dimpled potato nose and he wore a zip-up felt jacket.

Berryman spoke to the drunk. The two murmured back and forth. He was done with the students. Greer took out his wallet.

"I'll tell you one . . . thing," Berryman said. "The writer is slime."

"You're drunk," Greer said.

Berryman turned.

"I'll tell you why you write."

Greer was frightened.

Berryman said, "You went to a party one time. You were sort of maybe half invited. You spoke to a girl, and you felt like she ignored you. You spoke to another girl, and it seemed like she ignored you, too. Then a third girl ignored you. That's it. Everything spun from a habit you formed one night, at a party when you felt you were ignored. So don't you talk to me about imitation. Don't you talk to me about imitation."

"Let's go," Donald said.

"Sit down!" Berryman shouted. "Learn something!"

It was the last time either of the young men saw him. Later the same night Berryman was unable to get his key working in the door of his apartment. He woke up his landlord, singing, "I know that you hate me, John Lansman. You have hate in your heart." When his landlord refused to open the front door, Berryman pulled down his pants and defecated on the porch. He did not return to school. Later the boys learned that he had been fired.

After graduating, Greer was hired at Columbia. He went from assistant to associate professor quickly. At twenty-seven, he was on the campus-wide promotion and tenure committee.

He was still single. He went to bars looking for women. It was at the bar across from his office that he saw Donald, who sat alone in the corner fingering the lock on an expensive crocodile briefcase. Greer brought him a scotch.

"Monsieur le chef, salud!" Greer said.

Donald looked up and laughed. He explained that he had a job as a research assistant to an old woman who was writing a memoir about her father, a Hollywood producer. "A scion," Donald said. "These shitty memoirs are always about someone's famous great-grandmother."

"And your poetry?" Greer asked.

"I'm off it, fuck poems."

"I spend most of my energy on my students. C'est la vie."

"Yeah, well." Donald tipped back his drink. "You know any parties?"

Greer did know of some faculty parties. At the first party, in the English department, Donald drank several water glasses full of scotch. It didn't seem to affect him at all, except that his mood brightened. When the party began to wind down, Greer took Donald to a second party around the corner, where Donald switched to red wine. After midnight, he buttonholed the host's wife.

"Ish like my frien the great John Berryman tole me. You . . . The man taught me to be honesh. Alienation . . . We lie to our parents, and we tell them, 'I love you.' But really I jus want her money when she dies. I want her stone mashion. I lie to my frensh. I say this work is promising. I lie to my colleagues, same way. My bosh. Ish really promising. Someone shows me a DOG TURD! An I say, you know, ish really promising. You know how it ish. Course you do, you're a woman."

The professor's wife was nervous. She said, "Well, that's interesting. I think we've all—"

Donald railroaded her.

"I'll be honesh. William Shawn, if you want my opinion, is a faggot. That's my opinion, if I can be honesh. I had a tremendoush hard-on. Just like steel, I mean, lishen. We men—"

Greer suggested they go downtown to a bar he knew, where they could dance. When the bar closed, Donald was angry. He didn't want to go home, and so they took a cab to Greer's. Donald was sobering up.

Greer said, "Can I tell you something? And you can't make fun of me?"

"Of course."

"There's a bakery downstairs. It opens at seven, but if I knock on the door they'll usually let me in. Some late nights I go down and get a cookie."

"I'd love a cookie!" Donald said. "I could eat a whole cake."

Down in the bakery, Greer picked a half dozen cookies, pointing through the steamed glass, while Donald blew into his hands and stomped his feet. When they were paying, Donald pointed out a six-layer chocolate cake with ganache icing and slivered almonds pressed to the side.

He said, "And that."

As the woman boxed the cake, a blue child's birthday cake caught Greer's eye. He pointed to it. "Did you ever have one of those when you were a kid? I always wanted one of those."

"Get it. Why not?"

Upstairs, the two men sat on Greer's bed—Greer didn't have a table, he didn't usually have guests—and they took turns with Greer's fork, eating their separate cakes.

Greer said, "I really like Valentino Bucchi."

"Who?"

Greer put on the pianoforte album. Donald stood up after a few bars and said, "It's terrific!" He danced around Greer's apartment, acting out the moods of the songs—by turns longing and monstrous. When Greer fell asleep he was still doing it.

At sunrise Donald was fast asleep beside Greer. The mattress was bowed by his weight, and he had kicked the sheet down, so the wool blanket was on his skin. Greer lifted the blanket and pulled up the sheet for Donald. Then he slipped out of bed.

When Greer returned to his apartment later that day, he

noticed that Donald had left his briefcase behind. He opened it and found a manuscript. It wasn't the memoir about the old woman's famous father. It was about a society of men.

Greer was jealous. He sat at his own typewriter and began to write. He imagined another world, one like this one, but more. In this world there were only men. Close to midnight he looked up from his typewriter.

"I have something here," he said.

Donald never called about the briefcase, and after hanging on to it for a few months, Greer thought it was best to throw it away.

Mensworld was stuck in edits. Greer's first editor left the company, and his second suggested that they begin again. "Let's not be afraid to get our hands dirty."

And then something awful happened. Donald hadn't given up on his novel. He had just begun fresh. Or maybe it had already sold. Greer didn't know. He just saw fifty copies of *Boys Boys Boys* by Donald Burdon sitting in the window of a bookstore. Then he read the rave in the *Times*. Then he saw Donald on the cover of a magazine. He wore a beautiful white jacket, and had his arm around Gore Vidal's shoulders.

Greer's book came out quietly, during Donald's paperback release. At Greer's book party—an elegant affair, held in Philosophy Hall—his students stood and knocked their fists against the tables.

When students asked him about Donald Burdon, Greer

deflected. He told them the story about Berryman in the bar, which always got a laugh.

Greer took no satisfaction in it when Donald couldn't handle success. There were those people who did, who cravenly traded in "Donald stories." Greer always did his best to defend Donald. But he knew Donald better than anyone else, and so he often had the best stories. "Donald had explosive diarrhea on the way to the bathroom at Elaine's and refused to go home." "Donald developed a painful, public, unrequited crush on Susan Sontag, and showed up on her doorstep morning after morning to recite Florentine verse." "Donald mailed William Shawn flowers each Monday, along with contrite apologies for 'the thing about your penis.'"

Once, Donald woke Greer close to 4 a.m., banging on his door, shouting, "I want to reach out to you with honeyed hands."

Greer pulled his head inside and closed his window very slowly.

Several years after his first book, Donald took a teaching position in Ireland. And then for a few years, the only peep from Donald was an occasional book review. He was like an angry bear who only came out of his cave to tear bestselling books to pieces. If something was doing well, if it was regarded as a work of art, then you could count on a blistering essay from Donald.

Greer rarely heard from him. For months, he forgot that there had ever been an alligator briefcase with a manuscript inside it. Had he stolen anything at all? Wasn't all writing, all so-called inspiration, just borrowing?

Then Donald came back to the city.

Greer made his mistake. He felt guilty. He started singling Donald out for praise. When he was asked publicly to name his favorite writer, he eulogized Donald. Then he hired Donald for a visiting appointment at Columbia.

And now, on the first day of the semester, Donald had already been disruptive.

"Thank you, Guillermo," Greer said. "That was very helpful. Okay, well. If there's nothing else."

Greer was about to wrap up the meeting.

Donald raised his hand.

"Professor Burdon," Greer said. "Yes, Professor Burdon, uh."

Donald lowered his hand. He stood up. He held the floor in silence for a long time. His raincoat was bunched at the elbows. His eyebrows were long and wild. He looked out from under them, at the students and faculty. Then he said, "Do you remember the night we went to a donkey show together?"

"Donald. If that's all, I think we've concluded the meeting."

"For those who don't know, this is when a woman is having sex with a donkey. Don't go, everyone," Donald said. "It sounds good, but in reality it's just gross. Ben knows what's coming. Don't you? I wanted to kill myself, Ben. Valentino Bucci was on the radio."

Greer looked at the other faculty members, trying to

silently form a coalition. Surely Donald wouldn't accuse him in front of his peers. But Donald had them.

"I wanted to kill myself, and it was all because of you. Do you know how little I had? I had nothing. I had nothing. And then through hard work and toil—blood and tears—I manage to shape something, and then you saw it, all formed, and you stole it. You think because I didn't say anything that you got away with it, and nobody knew?" He looked slowly around the room. "You built your house on a lie. You're a liar, Benjamin. You're a thief. You're a mediocrity. And everyone here"—he gestured grandly around the room—"everyone here knows it." Then he took a small bow and sat down.

Greer had dreaded these words for so long. When they were spoken, and in the nightmarish context, he was surprised to see the effect they had, of making their speaker look ridiculous. Someone coughed. A couple of his students snickered.

All Ben had to do was adjourn the meeting.

Rinpoche

My mom and I were in the apartment we shared in Seattle. It was summer. It was the middle of June. I was sitting on the couch looking out the window and my mom was in the kitchen making bone broth. She was going through a phase of making pho. She had made a pho and brought it into work, and it confused her that nobody ate it.

My mom's cell phone rang. I held it up and said, "It's Jim."

She wiped her hands and took the phone out of my hands. She said, "What's up?" into the phone. I heard Jim ask her how she was doing.

When she got off the phone, she was jealous. She said Jim told her Rinpoche had called him. Jim and Rinpoche had an hour-long conversation, according to Jim, whose wife, Eileen, was sick. He never talked about it. His wife was sick, and she'd had two knee surgeries over the winter, and she'd continued to work through most of it. She drove a school bus. It was a part of her job to put the chains onto the tires. Jim never told anybody about Eileen, really, and so people had decided she was going to be all right.

It was complicated because there were two sick people in Seattle. One of them, Carole, was dying. She had a tube in her stomach that drained the fluid out. Her face had changed. It had gotten thin, so that it looked like a skull. She went in and out of consciousness. I mean, she slept and woke up. When she was awake, she was never gone, but her conversation was confused and she was emotional. The emotion that she felt most powerfully was wanting. It was so powerful and so insane when it came over her that it riled people up. It came over them.

That was my impression at the time. Later I found out that people had donated money to Carole, and my mother had spent it on us. She hadn't done anything extravagant, but she had used it for us. She reasoned that it was less than what she'd spent taking care of Carole, and that was true. Really, it was awful what was happening to Carole. She'd gotten cancer in a three-year retreat. She had travel insurance, but they denied her claim. She didn't know—as many people don't—that you can't take no for an answer in a situation like that. She accepted it, for a while, and the cancer grew. Later she had trouble taking her medications. She was prescribed a medication that broke the cancer up, but it made her feel bad. She said it was poison. So she'd take it irregularly. That let the cancer spread. Then we had a big meeting coming up—something a lot of people would go to—and Carole wanted to look good. She took some psylium husk, and it collapsed her stomach, and that was how it happened, really. She was going to die.

A lot of people came to visit Carole now that she was dying, but my mom was the one who visited the most. For this reason, and because my mother had spent her money, though I didn't know that at the time, Carole had come to hate my mother. There was also an iPad. Rinpoche had given Carole an iPad, and Carole gave it to my mother. But the story she told people was that my mother had taken it. This is how it is when people are dying. I barely ever visited. Once, I went with a couple of other people. One person massaged Carole's feet and said, "How do reincarnation and emptiness make sense together?"

She meant, if it is a dream, if it is empty, then why do we die and turn into dogs. I was quiet and then I said, "They are one." I meant reincarnation and emptiness are one. The woman who'd asked was about fifty. She was a powerful, intelligent woman. She nodded. She nodded in the way you nod if someone has said something stupid. I said, "What I meant was that it is like dreaming through the night—having all different dreams." For some reason I was shaking. I was sure my answer was correct, according to Buddhist philosophy, but more recently I learned the correct answer, which is a bit subtler.

The woman made a little more conversation. We got onto the subject of Sikkim, in India, where Rinpoche had been taken after he was recognized in Bhutan. She said in his room, on the walls, you could see scratch marks from his tantrums.

"What do you mean?" I asked, and she said, "He clawed the walls because he didn't want to have to study. He wanted to be an ordinary boy and go play with all the others." Later I saw a still from a film by Satyajit Ray. It was Ray's documentary on Sikkim. He had filmed Rinpoche at four or five. In the still, Rinpoche had a long face that came to the point of his chin, and he wore a five-pointed crown. He was scowling at the camera like an old man.

Rinpoche had asked to stay with Jim in Seattle, but Jim had told him that he didn't have room. Also, Jim said his place wasn't right, because of the floors.

Jim was an editor. He did carpentry as a hobby. Several years earlier, he had lifted up the floors in his condo, planning to lay down hardwood, but the job was too big. And then he had gotten accustomed to concrete.

He saw himself as the senior student in the Seattle *sangha*. My mother hosted all the get-togethers at her apartment—when we'd meet to recite a *sadhana*, or have a *tsok*—and she had been a Buddhist as long as Jim. She didn't ever say she saw herself as the senior student, and she didn't ever act like she ought to be the senior student, but if anyone else tried to act senior, it offended her, and she undermined them. Jim in particular. Probably because he didn't like her, but also because the way he chanted was affected. People who have spent a great deal of time chanting learn the sound of their own voices. This sound is always different—sometimes it is very low, and sometimes it is sweet; sometimes it is metallic and sometimes it is sharp. Sometimes it is melodic. Often old Tibetan men chant very low, from their stomachs or below even that; often Western practitioners who have really practiced a lot pick up turns here and there that are melodic.

This melodic sound, in the *sangha* of Jim's first guru, had become a group quality, so that the students all embellished words here and there in certain ways. Jim chanted this way. He was the only one, and so rather than sounding beautiful, it was disruptive. It sounded aggressive. I don't think that he meant it that way, or if he did it, was so subtle only some people could hear it. But really it doesn't matter. It was how he chanted, and he was the chant leader. The proper etiquette was to follow him. But my mother didn't like it. She chanted her own way—very softly and very badly, often tripping over the words. She was extremely sensitive to tone. Bruce thought tone—the way he said my mother's name—was a silent weapon. He did not understand that his inflections stayed with her for weeks: he didn't like my mother. It was primarily because he was not attracted to her. There are other ways to say that. He didn't like my mother because she didn't groom herself well, and her house was dirty. He was clean. His house was clean, and he owned several blazers, and his skin always shone, but to my mother, none of this mattered. To her, he didn't have any taste. If my mom had cleaned, which she did not, then she would have cleaned better. My mom had once had money.

My mom, me, and my mom's friend Louise were standing in the front bedroom of my mom's apartment; we had begun to clean for Rinpoche's attendants. We were in my bedroom, which had an ocean view. Sea lions swam in the water. They had a funny habit of coming up four times for air and then going under again, and sometimes they barked. Twice I saw orca whales swimming through the water out front. One had a massive, ragged fin. It was so different than at Sea World in Austin. But the apartment was full of a decade of clutter.

Louise said, "It seems odd to put Rinpoche in Carole's apartment and put his attendants here."

My mom said, "Well, that's what Jim said."

"It's kind of stupid to give him the little apartment in back and put his attendants in yours with all this space and the view."

"Well, tell Jim that," my mom said.

I said, "Call him and tell him. He won't listen to us. Call him and tell him. When we say it, he won't listen. If you say it, he'll listen. Call him and tell him."

I repeated myself a few times.

Louise said, "I will."

"Because Rinpoche should be in here," I said. I pointed at the floor, meaning that he should be in my room.

"I think your mom's might make more sense," Louise said. "He hates the sound of motorcycles. He likes quiet."

"No," I said, "this is clearly the better room."

Louise's call changed it, and we began to really clean. I took all the bags and baskets and boxes and unopened mail and trash bags of pills and the dharma books, and the hundreds of audiocassette recordings of dharma lectures, and put them in a pile. It took about an hour. The pile covered the entire living-room floor. You could walk around it to get to the patio, or to the couch, but it was about twelve feet in diameter. It was evening, and looking at the pile, and all the mess that remained around it, I recognized the amount of work there was to be done. I was sure it could be done, but looking at the pile, I thought, It cannot be done.

The next day, my mother bought twenty-five moving boxes. I took every single thing out of the refrigerator and out of the cabinets—every cooking utensil, every exotic spice—and we went through them. The things she wanted to keep went into boxes, which we would take to storage later. The things she would throw away went into garbage bags. The nicer things that she did not want we put outside, and people took them away—for example, the meat slicer. She had too many expensive culinary supplies. We went on in this way, in each room, first clearing the clutter and then beginning to clean the surfaces. When the clutter had all been thrown away or boxed up and carried down, my mother hired a carpet cleaner, and he came and shampooed the carpets. He mentioned, on leaving, that I had quite a lot of hair. I began to clean the surfaces in each room, and my mother began to go and find—with economy—the small things that were needed to fill a space. She made several trips to her office, where she "borrowed" five armchairs, two standing lights, two patio chairs, a patio table, a desk, a coffee table, and several side tables.

Then she came home crying. Jim had called her on the phone while she was out.

"What did he say?"

"He said he doesn't know if Rinpoche can stay with us."

"What?"

"He said he wasn't sure about it."

"What did you say?"

"I said you can't turn around and change your mind. We've been working too hard. You can't just up and change it."

"What'd he say?"

"He said he had to think about it."

"Why?"

"He said, 'The clutter! The clutter!'" She imitated Jim's voice saying, "'The clutter.'"

"What clutter?" I said. "We're cleaning. Did you tell him we would clean it?"

"I told him that, and he said, '*How?!*'"

"What's he mean, how? You take it and you throw it out, that's how. Maybe he doesn't know—he is so busy buying fish at Costco."

My mother smiled.

"Remember that disgusting fish he served us? It looked like it had exploded."

"He said he was going to return it."

"Return a fish!"

"They do that, too, at Costco—they'll take anything back."

"But he couldn't have—he'd be ashamed to bring in some exploded salmon and a receipt."

"I'm sure he did it—brought that nasty thing in and got his twenty-five dollars. He kept saying, 'How are you going to clean in time?' and 'The clutter!'"

"I don't like that, the way he says your name."

"He's abusive. I've had the thought about him before, of just—he's abusive. To go and change his mind like that. Yes,

Rinpoche can stay with you; no, he's staying across the hall—
I'm in control and I'm the boss and you will do what I say
and it will be the way I say it is."

"Abusive."

"It's not physically abusive, but it's abuse. Getting our
hopes up. Look at all the work we did, and then—not even a
'no' but just an 'I'm not sure'—make sure we're still on the
line, working, sucking up—it's classic male abuse."

Five days went by. I had torn up the shelf paper in the kitchen
cabinets, taken each shelf down, washed and dried it, and
then cut new shelf paper to fit. I had thrown out everything
in the refrigerator and in the freezer, cleaned every shelf and
surface by removing the shelves and soaking them in hot, soapy
water, and then replaced them. I had moved the refrigerator
and the stove to clean and wash behind them, and scrubbed
the kitchen floor on my hands and knees. I had found a drain-
ing pan under the refrigerator full of mold, emptied it, cleaned
it, bleached it, and replaced it. I had removed everything from
the bathroom closet and all of the drawers, and wiped the
surfaces down, and scrubbed all the water fixtures and tiles
with a brush and grout cleaner. I cleaned the fireplace and took
the grate out to the grass to scrape it down with a razor. I
washed the windows, and buffed the heating ducts with steel
wool. My mother bought spray paint and repainted them
white, and we opened all the doors to air the fumes. Several
of the other Buddhists in Seattle came over to help us, but they
were disoriented—like people stepping into a new job—and

I was exhausted, and had taken control of the space, and had difficulty delegating. The place was completely clean, and they couldn't find anything to do. They came to me asking for suggestions. Then, when I made suggestions, they were offended—they did not want to take steel wool to the feet of the iron railing on the patio of my home. This was understandable. But now Carole's place, by comparison, which had seemed so clean and so un-in-need of work, presented itself by comparison, and I was too exhausted to begin, and two women from the *sangha* took over and did as I had done—carrying down what had seemed like no belongings, wiping surfaces that had appeared clean—and it took them two days, and by the end, they owned the territory of Carole's place as I owned the territory of my mom's apartment. It was a Friday afternoon, and I was alone. The women who had cleaned Carole's had gone for coffee, to celebrate their work, and my mother was gone, too. Jim was coming over to hang art on my mother's walls—a loan—and to rehang the doors of the closet in my room.

Jim noticed that the baseboards of one wall were not painted in the living room, and they were not painted in my mother's room. I had not even seen them. I did not even know it was something I had omitted. My mother had seen the flaw and asked me to paint several days before. I had agreed, but then I had ignored it, and I had not delegated it when I had the chance, so now Jim pointed it out.

He had paint in his truck, and a long device for doing baseboards. After he had hung the art, he went down to his trunk and brought up paint. Quickly, efficiently, he painted the baseboards in the living room. He had an attitude. I thought he had an attitude. To me it felt like he was thinking, I notice the details.

We had brought the closet doors up from storage for him to rehang. They were leaning against the wall in the front room. I think maybe it was just the way Jim moved through my mother's apartment—*my space*—like he owned it. I suddenly became enraged. Before he could paint the baseboards in my mother's bedroom, and before he could hang the closet doors, I told him, "Leave."

He said, "I don't think I will," and he went into the front room and I heard his power drill go. I was so enraged that I left. I went next door to Carole's apartment. I made myself a cup of tea. I found some pasta from the nice grocery store in her refrigerator—something my mom had bought—and I realized I had not been eating. I warmed it up and sat. I was shaking with rage. My hands were shaking violently. I ate a bite, then looked at the food, and hugged myself because I was shaking too much to enjoy the food.

The front door flew open. I heard two people, a man and a woman, going through the drawers of a credenza in Carole's living room. I couldn't hear what they were saying. Then one was standing in the kitchen. I knew him. It was David, a student of Rinpoche's from New York.

I felt like a cat burglar in Carole's house. I felt like a sneak—someone stealing. I said, "I'm never over here."

"Yeah, right," he said.

"This food is mine," I said. "My mother got it for me."

David's wife was in the other room. She said, "I found it,"

and she came into the hallway, where I could see her, but she was out of the room, behind her husband. In her hands was the iPad Rinpoche had given to Carole.

I said, "I'm pretty sure Carole gave that to my mom."

David said, "Carole can't read her phone."

I said, "Carole gave it to my mom. So before you take it, can you please remove my mom's email from it?"

David's wife said, "You can do that."

She brought me the iPad, but I was shaking, and I couldn't figure out how to delete my mom's email. They watched me struggle with it. I don't know what came over us, but the three of us were so angry. I was as angry as I have ever been. Later, when we saw each other, we apologized with our eyes. We never talked about it.

On his first two days in Seattle, Rinpoche stayed at a boutique hotel downtown. I heard later that right after he got to town, Carole called and said he needed to come to her hospital room. "He needs to come here now. I'm dying now."

Rinpoche and everyone piled into the van. The woman I mentioned, who massaged Carole's feet and thought I was dumb for saying that thing about reincarnation, was driving. They drove for a while, and then Rinpoche said, "You know, we don't have to go. She's fine." They turned around and went back to the hotel.

My mom and I were in our apartment. My mom was feeling left out. I was feeling astonished that Rinpoche was coming in two days, that he would be in our house.

Jim called my mom from the hotel bar.

"What?" my mom said.

He told her that he and Louise and Marc and Rinpoche were having a drink. He didn't invite her to join them. He just let her know it was happening. My mom hung up on him.

The phone rang again.

My mom answered. She was irritated, but she was also hopeful. She hoped that Jim and Louise and Marc had called her back to invite her to join them. They didn't. They'd just called to tease her. She hung up the phone again.

"What's going on?" I said.

She said, "Louise said, '*Why'd you hang up on Rinpoche.*' Real cute. They're all over there laughing, having a drink with Rinpoche."

Then I felt left out, too. It was strange to feel left out, when he would be at our house in thirty-six hours, but we felt that way. We felt like we had cleaned the place stem to stern. And now we were alone. What were we, the cleaning ladies? The help.

Rinpoche was in our living room. Even though it was clean, it sometimes had a funny smell, and so my mom and I had opened the sliding glass doors wide. A fierce ocean breeze whipped through the apartment. It whipped your hair around. After fifteen minutes, one of Rinpoche's attendants said, "Maybe we could close the door," and after that, we had dinner.

My mom and I didn't know how to serve Rinpoche. It was strange to have him sitting in our apartment at a table. When

I was a kid, I could do it easily, but now I was awkward. When he and his attendant had finished eating, I stumbled over to the table and blurted, "Are you done?"

I always had trouble serving. It was not because I resisted doing something for Rinpoche but because I sensed that he wanted me to be natural. I didn't know how to do that, and so I would get tongue-tied and completely strange.

The next day we went to an outdoor mall, and Rinpoche bought an adapter so he could play songs from his iPod in the car. He handed me the adapter and said, "Can you figure this out for me?" The instructions were extremely simple. They were intuitive. But I was dumbfounded, and twenty minutes later I turned to Rinpoche and said, "I can't understand it."

He screwed up his face and said, "You just put one end here and one in the car."

I shrugged.

That night at a Thai restaurant Rinpoche asked Jim and my mom why they had been fighting. They said they didn't know. He turned to me and asked, and I tried to think of the answer.

He said, "You should write a story about it."

He stayed four nights and we saw a lot of movies. We ate at TGI Friday's, and shopped at Banana Republic. During the daytime people came to have short interviews with him in our place, or we went shopping. On his last day, before we came back to the apartment for a potluck dinner, he said that it was time to go and see Carole. It was just me, my mom, and Rinpoche in the car. When we got to Carole's hospital door, I said, "We'll wait out here," but Rinpoche told us to come inside. Carole was happy to see him, and she didn't mind us anymore. Whatever it was between us had passed.

Rinpoche told Carole that when she died, she would think she had to do a lot of complicated things. She would want it to be harder than it was. He said she didn't need to do anything complicated; he said, "Just mere knowing," and something else. It was something that simple, and he repeated both over and over, to make sure they went into her head. She was less than a week from dying, and it was the last time I would ever see her. I went to New York a few days later, and we were on the phone when we said goodbye. I told her I was sorry I wasn't there. I said goodbye. She was distant by then. She said, "Goodbye." We knew we were really saying goodbye. After she died, Rinpoche told Bruce to go and buy a really nice vegetarian meal and burn it. He bought a bunch of vegetables from the grocery store and lit them on fire. I made fun of him at the time, but Carole probably liked that. She loved Bruce. We were in her room for twenty minutes, but it felt like two. In the parking lot I opened Rinpoche's car door for him. I did it because I was so grateful to know him, because it was so clear to me in that moment that everything he did was for other people. It was the natural thing to do.

Acknowledgments

Thank you Anna Stein, Jin Auh, Mitzi Angel, Emily Bell, and Susan Golomb for believing in these stories; Michiko, Ron, and Cheryl for the retreat cabin; Sam Chang and Lorin Stein for your wisdom and knowledge; "Larry," Mom, and most of all Clancy for saving my life.